MONTANA MAVERICKS

Welcome to Big Sky Country, home of the Montana Mavericks! Where free-spirited men and women discover love on the range.

LASSOING LOVE

After years away, some of Bronco's most memorable sons and daughters have returned to the ranch seeking a fresh start. But there are some bumps along the road to redemption. Expect the unexpected as lonesome cowboys (and cowgirls) discover if they've got what it takes to grab that second chance!

When Jace Abernathy rescued baby Frankie from a tragic fire, he had no idea how that little boy would change his life. Nurse Tamara Hanson has helped him learn to be a good dad, but she resists the obvious connection between them. They're both so stubborn, nothing short of a miracle will push these two together— which is where they are meant to be.

Dear Reader,

Don't you just love a man who never gives up?

Firefighting rancher Jace Abernathy is a great guy with a big heart—the first one to the rescue in any emergency, the one you can count on to come through no matter what. When Jace makes a promise, nothing will stop him from keeping it.

This time, he's promised to adopt an orphaned newborn. The task seems impossible. He's single and there are already plenty of hopeful couples waiting in line for a baby of their own.

Jace is going to need help with this one—from his family, from his community. And most of all, from a strong, determined nurse named Tamara Hanson, who's had it up to here with the males of the species. It's going to be a real challenge to get Tamara on his side.

But Jace just won't quit. No matter what, he's going to be that orphaned baby's dad. And while he's at it, he's determined to win a certain wary nurse's wounded heart.

I hope you root for Jace, that you get behind his can-do spirit as he finds a way to be a worthy dad to a baby who needs him—and the right man for a woman who's given up on love.

Happy reading, everyone!

Christine Rimmer

The Maverick's Surprise Son

CHRISTINE RIMMER

HARLEQUIN
SPECIAL
EDITION

Special thanks and acknowledgment are given to
Christine Rimmer for her contribution to the
Montana Mavericks: Lassoing Love miniseries.

Recycling programs
for this product may
not exist in your area.

ISBN-13: 978-1-335-72473-1

The Maverick's Surprise Son

Copyright © 2023 by Harlequin Enterprises ULC

For questions and comments about the quality of this book,
please contact us at CustomerService@Harlequin.com.

Harlequin Enterprises ULC
22 Adelaide St. West, 41st Floor
Toronto, Ontario M5H 4E3, Canada
www.Harlequin.com

Printed in U.S.A.

Christine Rimmer came to her profession the long way around. She tried everything from acting to teaching to telephone sales. Now she's finally found work that suits her perfectly. She insists she never had a problem keeping a job—she was merely gaining "life experience" for her future as a novelist. Christine lives with her family in Oregon. Visit her at christinerimmer.com.

Visit the Author Profile page at Harlequin.com for more titles.

This book is dedicated to Dotty Graves and her rescue Landseer Newfoundland, Luna, and also to Bree Kotolski and her boxer/Pyrenees mix, Bailey. Luna and Bailey are the dual inspirations for the hero's two rescue dogs in this story.

Dotty says, "Luna may have actually rescued me instead of me her. When I went to see her, she would not let me out of the gate. So, of course, I opened the back of my SUV and she jumped in."

As for Bailey, Bree explains, "She is honestly the sweetest dog I have ever met. She calms both of our kids if they are upset. She stays close to our daughter who has seizures. And she will ask for hugs, then carefully stand up on her hind legs when you agree to give her one."

Thank you, Bree and Dotty, for sharing your stories of Bailey and Luna with me and allowing me to use their names and descriptions in this book.

Chapter One

"Don't even think about it, Jace," muttered Billy, oldest of Jace Abernathy's four siblings. Divorced with three half-grown kids at home, Billy was the solid one, the both-feet-on-the-ground one. "Not every crying woman is your problem."

Jace gave Billy a nod. "Relax, big brother. I'm not budging from this stool."

Yes, the sobs of the blonde crying alone at the table in the corner did compel him to rush to her side, dry her tears and promise that whatever she needed, he would do what he could to help her get it.

But in the end, running to the rescue of down-hearted women had never ended well for Jace—or for the women he'd tried to save. Uh-uh. Today, he was keeping his butt firmly planted on the barstool and enjoying his beer.

Up long before dawn, Jace, Billy and their second-born brother, Theo, had spent the morning and early afternoon feeding livestock, burning ditches and baling alfalfa on the family spread, the Bonnie B. Once the day's work was done, they'd caravanned into town for a beer at everybody's favorite watering hole, Doug's.

Right now, Jace only needed to tune out the sad sound of the poor woman crying and to focus on the good things—his brothers beside him and a cold brew in front of him. They were having a fine time, too, bellied up to the bar, swapping stories with the bar's owner.

At eighty-eight, Doug Moore was sharp, fun and energetic as ever. He led the wide-ranging discussion, which covered a number of goings-on in town recently. They all agreed that Bronco, Montana's upcoming Fourth of July festivities were bound to be bigger than ever, and that the rodeo-riding Hawkins family's arrival in town last year had really livened things up.

Then Theo gestured at the roped-off stool next to the window at the end of the bar. "When are you going to get rid of that stool, Doug?"

Doug gave Theo his easy smile. "Never." The stool was not only roped off but marked with yellow caution tape and labeled with a sign that read Death

Seat. "The haunted stool is famous," the old man declared proudly. "Folks drop in just to get a look at it."

Billy scoffed. "It's famous because it brings bad luck to everyone who sits on it."

Doug shook his gray head. "Not everyone. Let me remind you that Bobby Stone, arguably the unluckiest man ever to sit on that stool—I mean, given that he died shortly afterward—has recently returned from the grave."

They all laughed at that. Bobby had reappeared in Bronco last winter very much alive.

"Yep." Doug flipped his bar towel onto his shoulder. "Life can surprise a man. You never know what might happen next."

From over in the corner came another soft, hopeless-sounding sob followed by a pitiful little sniffle. Jace took a slow breath and remained on his stool. No, he was *not* running to the rescue. But that didn't keep him from feeling concern for someone who was suffering. It bothered him a lot, to know someone was hurting and yet to do nothing about it.

Theo elbowed Billy and snickered. "Uh-oh. Looks like Jace is about to find true love. Again."

Jace shrugged off Theo's remark. Hard truth? He *had* been involved with more than one fragile, needy woman. But he wasn't doing that anymore. Next time he fell, it would be the real thing with someone strong and self-reliant.

And, anyway, Theo didn't know what he was talking about. Jace's concern for the woman across the room was not about romance. It was about someone in pain, which Jace couldn't bear—and Doug was watching him.

His resolve wavering, Jace met the bartender's wise dark eyes. "I think I'll go over there and check on her. Make sure she's all right."

As Theo grinned knowingly, Billy leaned across him to whisper, "Don't, Jace. Just don't."

Doug spoke up then. "She's okay, son—or she will be in time. Right now, she's just in love with a man who doesn't love *her*. She's leaving tomorrow, heading back to her hometown in Virginia, where she'll have her family around her to ease her broken heart."

"You're looking out for her till then?" Jace asked the older man.

"I am."

Jace believed him. Doug was a good man—and that urgent feeling Jace got in his chest when someone was in trouble? It eased.

He had a few errands to run before heading back to the Bonnie B, so he put some bills on the bar, thanked Doug and tipped his hat at his brothers.

Outside, the sky was a gorgeous expanse of endless blue, the temperature warm, but with a nice, cool breeze blowing down off the mountains. He jumped in his crew cab, rolled down all four windows, turned up the radio and headed for the feed store on Commercial Street.

He'd just rounded the corner onto Franklin Street and was feeling good, easy, not a care in the world—when that urgent feeling came on him again.

He sniffed the air blowing in the windows.

Smoke.

But coming from where?

Silencing the music, he slowed the pickup to a crawl. The residential street lined with small one-story houses seemed peaceful. A skinny kid on a bike rode past going the other way, waving, giving Jace a big, gap-toothed smile.

Nothing to be concerned about, he thought. No sirens. No alarms. He almost turned the music back on.

But then he spotted the smoke. It billowed out a ground-floor window of a two-story, outside-access apartment building on the far side of the next corner.

A strange sort of calm settled over him. His heart-rate accelerated, but his mind was absolutely clear. Smoke meant fire, and he'd started training to be a firefighter when he was fourteen years old.

He heard the shriek of a smoke alarm as he swung around the corner and entered the parking lot behind the building. Waking his phone, he used the special app to contact the station where he volunteered weekly and was pretty much always on call.

As he rattled off information to the dispatcher, he swiped off his hat and dropped it on the passenger seat. He also took his pager off his belt and stuck it in the glove box. When it started beeping, it would only distract him from the job at hand. He had a fire extinguisher mounted under his seat. But judging by the volume of smoke boiling out that window, his extinguisher wasn't big enough to put out this fire.

Jumping from the cab, he ran for the building. The crew would be there ASAP. But too often, ASAP was not soon enough. He stayed on the phone with the dispatcher, reporting what he saw as he knocked loudly on the apartment door.

No answer. He could hear the smoke alarms going off in a couple of the other units now, too.

And the smell of smoke was stronger. People in other parts of the six-unit building were running out, shouting warnings to each other, slamming doors, yelling, "Fire! Call 911!" Feet pounded down the outside stairs.

But from beyond the door where the fire burned? Crickets.

The door was cool to the touch. Jace put his phone on speaker, told the dispatcher he was going in and shoved his phone in his pocket. On a call, the absolute rule was two in, two out—you went in with your partner and came back out as a team.

But now it was just him, with no time to waste. He tried the doorknob. Miraculously, it swung open. An orange tabby cat darted between his legs and raced off, disappearing around the corner of the building. He stepped into a sparsely furnished, smoky living room.

To his left, an arch led to a square of hallway and what looked like maybe a bedroom and bath. No smoke back there. Instead, it rolled toward him through the archway on the opposite wall that led into what he assumed was the kitchen.

"Bronco Fire and Rescue!" he shouted over the blare of the smoke alarms. "Anybody here?"

He heard coughing from somewhere in all that smoke followed by a strangled cry. "Help!" The voice sounded female. "In here!"

"On my way!" Dropping to his knees to get under the smoke, he crawled toward the arch and into the room, where the smoke was so thick he couldn't spot the woman who'd called out to him.

But then, to the continued blare of the fire alarm, convulsive coughing erupted to his left. Between coughs, the woman cried, "My baby! My baby's coming now!"

"Stay down, ma'am. I'm right here." He scuttled toward her. She was still coughing—hell, so was he. Right now, he'd give just about anything for his turnout gear.

"My baby!" she cried again. "My baby! Oh, no!"

He found her shoulders. She was on her back, clutching her belly. "It's okay," he lied. "I'm getting you out of here."

"Oh, dear God," was her only answer.

He said slowly, "Okay, we're staying low. Just—" his throat locked up and he coughed some more. "—

relax. Go limp. I'm going to drag you out by taking you under the arms…"

"He's coming!" the woman screamed. "I can't stop him. I'm having him right now." She said something else through another fit of coughing.

He slid one hand under each of her arms and then scrambled backward toward the arch. She struggled in his hold at first, groaning and coughing, crying out, "Oh, no! Oh, dear God…"

"Easy now," he said, trying to sound soothing even over the constant scream of the smoke alarms.

Finally, she seemed to get the message. She stopped fighting him and let him do the work.

At least the place was small. He dragged her across the living room and out the front door quickly. Rising, he reached over her to pull the door shut behind them.

The woman, in only a soot-streaked tank top and panties, was so young—in her teens, he'd bet. She rolled to her side. Clutching her big belly, she vomited right there on the welcome mat.

He should check the other units, make sure everyone had gotten out. But he couldn't leave this poor girl lying here. From what the dispatcher had told him, he judged arrival of the crew to be maybe ten minutes out. As a rule, when they sent a unit, they sent an ambulance. But he had to be sure.

As the girl cried and clutched her belly, he

whipped his phone from his pocket again. "Now!" the girl shouted. "He's coming right now!"

Jace asked for an ambulance. The dispatcher promised that one was on the way, his voice almost drowned out by the woman's screaming.

"Stay on the line," the dispatcher instructed.

"Roger that." He shoved the phone in his pocket again. Then he bent, scooped the poor girl up into his arms, surged to his feet and headed for his truck. She clutched him in a death grip and howled all the way.

Turned out, the situation was every bit as urgent as she'd repeatedly insisted. When he managed to fling the rear passenger door open and lay her down across the back seat, he could see that things had progressed a lot farther than he ever would have guessed.

As gently as possible, he eased off her panties.

The baby's head had already crowned.

The girl screamed as he informed her that he had EMT training—he did—and knew what he was doing—he hoped. He sent a silent prayer heavenward that his reassurances might prove true. He'd never delivered a baby alone before, but he'd helped out at the emergency birth of more than one. He'd also delivered a number of foals and several calves, as well.

As the girl cried and begged him to save her baby, he got out his first aid kit. He cleaned his hands and the cut on her head as best he could with wipes, then pulled on nitrile gloves. He spoke to her soothingly as the width of the baby's shoulders slowed the process momentarily and the young mother screamed bloody murder.

"Breathe," he begged her. "You're doing great."

And she was. Really, it seemed to be going well enough—and so damn fast.

Meanwhile, to the accompaniment of the never-ending warnings from the smoke alarms inside the burning building, the girl alternately shrieked, moaned, panted and talked. She babbled out a rambling story about going into labor hours before. When she'd called her doctor, he'd said it was too early to go to the hospital yet, so she'd been timing her contractions. She'd texted a girlfriend who was supposed to drive her to the hospital when the time came but got no answer, and when she'd called, it went to voice mail. And then she'd gotten hungry and decided to fry up some ground beef.

Somehow, she'd tripped—over her cat, she thought—and knocked herself out. "And when I came to, the room was on fire and the contractions were—" She started screaming again as the baby's shoulders popped free at last.

A moment later, as sirens wailed, coming closer, the rest of the baby's body slid right out. The baby—a boy—looked fine and strong, with ten fingers and ten toes. He opened his little mouth and let out an angry cry. Clearly, the newborn was furious to be suddenly shoved out into the big, bright world.

Jace heard whispering. Holding the infant, careful of the still-connected umbilical cord, he glanced over his shoulder and saw that there were people standing nearby. They all looked kind of lost, their faces dazed and bewildered.

A tired-looking middle-aged woman stepped forward and handed him a large white bath towel. "For the baby," she said softly. "Or the mom." She offered a small bottle of water, too. Holding the newborn in one arm, he managed to take the water and the towel with his free hand.

"The fire truck and the ambulance are on the way," he promised them all—as if they couldn't hear that for themselves. "Did everyone get out of the building?"

The tired-looking woman nodded, and a couple of others confirmed, "Yes."

Behind him in the crew cab, the new mother moaned. "My baby…"

He turned back to her, and she reached out her arms.

Dropping the bottle of water to the floormat, he draped the big towel over the girl's bare lower body. Then, carefully, he bent and laid the little boy on her chest. She wrapped her arms around him, kissed his gooey head and began whispering to him softly.

Jace picked up the water bottle again and unscrewed the cap. Gently, he cradled the woman's head with his free hand and offered her a drink.

Looking up at Jace through anxious eyes, she managed a couple of careful sips.

"Please, mister." She shook her head when he tried to coax her to drink a little more. He gently eased her head down to the seat again. As he screwed the cap back on the bottle, she stroked her baby's head and said to Jace, "I can see you're a good guy." Her voice was weak, breathless. "If something happens to me, you… You have to take him. You have to… take my baby."

He blinked and fell a step back. That wild, desperate look in her eye reminded him too sharply of the promise he'd made last year in a situation scarily similar to this—and that promise?

It was one he hadn't been able to keep.

"No!" he practically shouted. Gulping in a calming breath, he lowered his voice. "Really. Nothing's going to happen to you. You're going to be—"

"Please. I'm all he has. Don't let them put him in the system. You take him. Take him, please. Give him…a real home. Please."

"Listen, I really can't—"

"And my cat…" She talked right over him. "He's an orange tabby. His name is Morris. I need you to, um… make sure he's okay."

Jace felt sick to his stomach, but he sucked it up and reassured her yet again that she would be fine and she'd be a wonderful mom, that everything would work out right, that he'd seen the cat run out and Morris wasn't hurt.

But come on. What good did his promises and reassurances do? Bad stuff happened, and all the well-meaning promises in the world couldn't change that. He couldn't swear he would be able to find her cat.

And as for the baby...

Uh-uh. No. Even if he were willing to take on a newborn baby, he was in no position to guarantee that he could make that happen.

Which was why his answer to this poor girl had to be no. No more promises he wasn't sure he could keep. No way. Never again.

"You're going to be fine. Your little boy is fine. There's no need to worry about—"

"Oh!" The woman moaned. "Something is not right..." She let out a cry and shut her eyes as her arms went limp.

He dropped the water bottle and caught the baby before the little guy rolled off her chest to the floor.

The white towel? All of a sudden it was soaked with blood, like a dam had broken inside that poor girl.

Dear God in heaven, this was beyond bad.

He always tried to be prepared for anything. He always kept his first aid kit handy in his truck, along with extra rope, a seat belt cutter and a window punch—and that fire extinguisher under the front seat.

But postpartum hemorrhage? He recognized it, yeah, but that didn't mean he was prepared to deal with it.

Where was the damn Pitocin when a man needed it?

She opened her eyes. "Please. Please, mister... Take my baby... And my cat. You have to..." Her weak voice trailed off.

Now she'd gone really pale, a gray sort of pale. She was clammy with sweat. Carefully, he lifted the towel. There was a lot of blood with no sign of the placenta. He should at least try abdominal massage, to see if that might help.

He turned to look for someone to hold the baby— and the pumper pulled into the driveway, the ambulance right behind it.

The woman kept begging and the blood kept flowing. And then the sirens went silent. But the smoke alarms never stopped.

"Please," the woman chanted. "Take my baby, please. Find my cat..."

The situation broke him. He heard himself agree— to take the little boy he now held in his arms. To find the damn cat.

"He's an orange tabby," she whispered raggedly. "His name is Morris. Find him, please."

The baby shrieked in his ear. Jace cradled him close and rocked him side to side. He said, "I saw your cat run out. Honestly, I'm sure he's fine."

And then Livia Court, a paramedic from the ambulance crew, came rushing toward them. She asked for a quick update from Jace and he gave it. Then, speaking softly to the new mother, she clamped the cord and cut it.

"How's the baby?" asked Livia.

Jace replied, "Doing well." Still holding the crying newborn, Jace moved out of the way as RayAlvarez, the other paramedic, ran up with a stretcher. They swiftly loaded the new mother onto it and wheeled her toward the waiting ambulance.

The stunned and staring people from the building had stepped back. The pumper crew was already rolling out lines to deal with the fire.

Jace cradled the naked, screaming baby closer. At least the day was warm. The little guy wasn't shivering—just in desperate need of his mother in this big, scary new world he'd fallen into.

Continuing to rock him, Jace whispered, "Okay, now. It's okay. Everything is going to be okay. They are going to fix your mama up just fine." As if words helped. As if saying them could make them true.

Miraculously, the baby quieted. Jace cradled his blood-streaked head and held him away a bit to look at him. The little one stared up at him almost in wonder, his tiny mouth working, as though he was trying to figure out what that hole was doing in his own face.

Jace felt a laugh bubbling up. He swallowed it down. There was nothing to laugh about here.

And then Sharon Cox, one of other firefighters whom they all called ZipIt because she never did, came running from the ambulance. "They're ready for him now," she said. "I'll take him."

He passed the little guy over. His arms suddenly way too empty, he asked, "The mother?"

"We're doing everything we can." Sharon's grim expression was not reassuring. For once, even ZipIt seemed to have very little to say. They shared a glance of bleak understanding.

And then she was turning, striding for the ambulance, cradling the baby who had started wailing again.

Jace was left standing there alone. He watched the ambulance race away, siren screaming. Shoving the back seat door shut on the bloody mess and that crumpled, red-stained towel, he went to do what he could to help put out the fire.

A half hour later, the blaze was extinguished, and the smoke alarms silenced. The young mother's apartment had been gutted, and the one above it was almost as bad.

"The center units have smoke damage," said the chief, Dan Foster, aka DantheMan. "Only the front two apartments got away clean—but the baby is safe and the mother is at the hospital by now." The older man clapped him on the shoulder. "Good work, Junior."

Every firefighter Jace knew had a nickname. Jace got his back when he was fourteen—and not because he was named after his dad. He wasn't. But when he was eight years old, a bad barn fire out at the ranch had killed his dog, Ginger. That day, Jace had vowed to become a firefighter when he grew up. And as soon as he was old enough, he'd started volunteering at the station as a junior firefighter.

The older guys had called him Junior from the first day and never stopped. He would carry that nickname to his grave.

Jace said, "The woman's cat is missing. Anybody happen to see an orange tabby? A good-sized cat. His name is Morris."

DantheMan shook his head. "Not that I know of, but I'll ask around."

Jace knew he should follow the pumper back to the station and help out. They were a limited crew, most of them volunteers. There was always way too much work to do after a fire.

But first, he had to know for certain that the mother and the baby were okay. "I have to check on something," he told the chief. "But I'll stop by the station after."

With another firm clap on his shoulder, the chief let him go.

Jace marched to his crew cab and got up behind

the wheel. He yanked off his bloody nitrile gloves and threw them over his shoulder into the carnage of the back seat.

For a minute, he just sat there, staring blindly out the windshield, thinking about that promise he'd made, telling himself he would not have to keep it. The young mother would be fine. She would recover and raise her son.

And once things settled down, the orange cat named Morris would show up, none the worse for wear.

At Bronco Valley Hospital, the fiftyish woman behind the glass partition in reception eyed Jace warily.

He couldn't really blame her. He'd spent a few minutes in the restroom just now, cleaning up as best he could. But his T-shirt and jeans remained covered in soot, ashes and streaks of dried blood. Plus, he smelled like a doused house fire, like burned wood and soggy, half-incinerated upholstery with acrid hints of melted plastic.

He tried his best to look harmless as he gave the woman his name. "I'm Jace Abernathy, ma'am." In Bronco, people respected the Abernathy name as a rule, though this woman did not seem particularly impressed. He put on a regretful expression. "Sorry I'm such a mess, but I volunteer at Bronco Fire and Rescue. I just came from that fire over on Franklin Street. And I'm here because I delivered the baby the ambulance brought in not too long ago. I just wanted to check on them—the baby and the mother. I wanted to make sure they're both all right."

The woman gave him a careful smile. "Hold on just a minute, will you?"

"Uh, yeah. Sure. Thank you."

She rose from her swivel chair and went through a door behind her. When she came back out she said, "Please have a seat, Mr. Abernathy. A nurse will be with you shortly."

"All right, but I just want to know—"

"Please," she cut him off. And she wasn't quite meeting his eyes. What was she not saying? "The nurse will tell you whatever you need to know. Just sit over there. It won't be long, I promise you."

He gave up and went to the waiting area a few feet away, where all the chairs were upholstered in fresh-looking nubby fabric. Not wanting to dirty up the furniture, he stayed on his feet.

Time crawled. He had a bad feeling and that made him antsy. He kept glancing at the round clock on the wall over the reception desk. Three minutes went by—minutes that felt like half a century.

And then, from down a long hallway, a short, very pretty brunette in light blue scrubs bustled toward him. She had her shoulders back and her head high. When she spotted him, she smiled—a forced smile.

His heartrate accelerated.

The news was not good. He was certain of that now.

The nurse's big brown eyes locked with his as she rounded the shoulder-high wooden partition that screened off the waiting area. "Mr. Abernathy?"

"Jace. Please."

"Jace. Hi. I'm Tamara Hanson." She gestured at the nearest chair. "Have a seat."

He glanced down at his filthy T-shirt and sooty jeans. "I'd better not."

"Please don't worry about that." She indicated the empty chair again.

He didn't budge except to stick his hands in his pockets. Quietly, he explained, "I just want to know about the woman and the baby from the Franklin Street apartment fire. I got them out and delivered the baby in the back of my truck, and now I just need to know how they're doing."

"Mr…" Before he could correct her, she caught herself. "Jace." Another forced smile. "The baby is fine. He's been fed special formula, and now he's napping in our neonatal intensive care unit."

"NICU?" Jace's gut clenched. "But you just said—"

"I'm sorry. I wasn't clear. Most babies stay in the room with their mothers. When that's not possible, we have a well-baby area in our small NICU."

He drew a slow, calming breath. "*Well baby*, you said." He savored the words. "Then he really is okay?"

"Yes. He is. He's just fine."

"And the mother?"

She pressed her full lips together. "I really think you ought to sit down."

His heart knocked hard in his chest, like a big fist trying to beat its way free of containment. He stood taller. "Talk to me, Tamara. Please just tell me the truth."

With a sad little sigh, she gave in. "I'm so sorry, Jace. The mother didn't make it."

Chapter Two

His knees went to jelly. The nearest chair beckoned him to collapse into it.

Jace braced his boots apart and stood firm. Quietly, he informed the pretty nurse, "I need to see the baby."

"You're upset, understandably so, and I think you ought to take a moment and—"

"I need to see the baby now!" He didn't realize he was shouting until Tamara flinched. The security guy stationed by the door turned and started toward them.

But the nurse put up a hand and shook her head at the guard, who stopped in his tracks.

She turned those big eyes on Jace again. There was fire in those eyes. Fire and sympathy and determination, too. She was petite and so sweet looking, but he saw true toughness in her. He knew that she would try one more time to get him to sit down, to listen to her sympathetic noises—after which she would herd him out the door.

And he would go.

Soon.

But not yet. Not till he'd reassured himself that the baby really was okay.

He lowered his voice and spoke to her softly, keeping the conversation just between the two of them. "Look. I made a promise to that baby's mother. I promised that I would look after her little boy."

The nurse's big eyes widened. "But it's not your responsibility to—"

"The mother, she was crystal clear. She doesn't want that little boy ending up in the foster care system. She said she was all the family that baby has."

Tamara lifted her hand and started to clasp his arm—but caught herself before making contact. She covered the move by smoothing a few strands of hair that had escaped her pinned-back hair. "Jace, you don't have to worry about him. He's healthy. He's fine. Truly. We're taking good care of him."

"I'm sure you are. But I... Look, I need to see for myself that the little guy's okay. Can't I just see him, just for a moment?"

The nurse's determined expression softened—damn, she really was pretty. With a sigh, she said gently, "Of course, you can see him. This way."

She led him back the way she'd come, through the double doors and along another hallway to a shut door, where she stopped and faced him. "You won't be able to hold him."

He looked down at his dirty T-shirt and soot-stained jeans. "I understand."

"If you'll wait right here, I'll bring him out."

"Okay, great."

She went through the door, which swung silently shut behind her. He stood there, hands at his sides, feeling like a walking germ factory.

A husky, graying man in brown scrubs came through the next door down the hall. Pausing at the sight of Jace, he asked warily, "Can I help you?"

"I'm waiting for Tamara Hanson." He pointed at the door she'd gone through. "She's in neonatal care and said she'd be right out."

"Ah," was the reply. The guy turned and headed for the nurses' station at the end of the long hallway.

To Jace's relief, Tamara emerged a moment later, a bundled baby in her arms. With a tender smile, she stepped close. He looked down at the little guy, who was sound asleep, his small face scrunched up, like it took real concentration just to sleep.

The nurse said softly, "He's fine. Full term. Twenty-one inches, eight pounds, twelve ounces. Apgar score of 8. That means he's healthy."

From his EMT training, Jace already knew that an Apgar score of 7, 8 or 9 usually meant the newborn was doing great. He looked down at the tiny little guy in Tamara's arms and really wanted to hold him, to whisper to him, *Don't you worry, little fella, I'm here. I won't let you down. Whatever it takes, I'll keep my promise to your mama.*

Instead, he kept his mouth shut and his hands at his sides. "I, uh…" He looked up at the nurse. She gave him a gentle smile. "Thank you," he said.

Sympathy flashed in her eyes. For a weird moment, they stared at each other, and he found himself wishing she would never look away. But then she blinked and glanced down at the baby. "Well," she said briskly with a too-bright smile. "As you can see, he's healthy. He's going to be fine." Damn straight he would be fine. Jace would make sure of that. "I'll just put him back in his bassinet."

And that was it. The nurse and the sleeping little boy vanished through the door to the NICU.

She wasn't gone long. When she reached his side again, she gestured toward the door to reception. "I'll see you out."

"I have a few more questions."

"Sure." She nodded at a couple of technicians as they hurried past. "Let's just return to the waiting area."

"Fair enough." They walked out in silence and ended up back by the chairs he wasn't going to sit in.

"All right, then," she said. "What more can I help you with?"

"What happens next for the baby?"

"He'll be kept overnight for observation. After that, if his father or other family can't be found right away, social services will be coming for him. He'll be in foster care until they can locate his relatives."

Jace got that urgent feeling again. "But what if he *has* no family? The mother told me there was no one else. She begged me to take him, to give him a home. And I... Well, I'm willing to do that. I promised her I would." As the words escaped his lips, he could hardly believe he was saying them—announcing out loud that he wanted a stranger's baby to raise. And he wasn't done yet. "How about if *I* just foster him to start?"

"Jace, I'm afraid it's not that simple. Applying to be a foster parent takes several months. There are multiple steps to the process."

"Okay, then. I'll do what I have to do."

Tamara shook her head. "I'm sorry. I don't know what more to tell you. And right now, I really need to..."

He put up a hand. "You're right, okay? I get it. You can't stand here reassuring me all day long."

"Well, it's just that I don't know what else to say."

Neither did he. He nodded. "Thank you again." He turned for the door.

Outside, the sun was still shining. He marched to his truck and got up behind the wheel. He'd done what he could for now. And he still needed to stop by the feed store and head for the station.

But when he left the parking lot, he turned his pickup back toward Franklin Street instead.

A few minutes later, he was pulling into the driveway behind the dead mother's burned-out apartment. Stopping off to the side so tenants could get in and out of the carports, he spotted a middle-aged blonde woman and a heavyset balding man standing on the concrete walkway that led out of the parking area toward the front of the building.

He recognized the woman. Roxy James was a reporter. She worked for the local paper, the *Bronco Bulletin*. She'd interviewed him last year, after he'd pulled an unconscious man from his burning ranch house. The man, Revell Courtney, had lived. His ten-year-old son had not.

"Jace Abernathy!" Roxy had spotted him. "Just the man I want to talk to."

He had little desire to answer the reporter's questions and even less to have to read his own words later in the *Bulletin*. But she just might have news about the orange tabby named Morris—the one he'd promised to find at the same time he'd vowed to adopt the now-orphaned newborn.

He went on over there. And a good thing, too. The man Roxy was interviewing turned out to be the building's landlord.

Roxy turned her sharp eyes on Jace. "I have a few questions." She fired them off like bullets.

Jace answered as simply and quickly as possible. After explaining how he'd come to be on Franklin Street at just the right moment and describing how he'd pulled the young mother from her burning apartment, he added, "Listen, Roxy. I don't mind answering all your questions. But I want some information from you in return."

Roxy nodded. "I get your story and you can have what I know."

The landlord spoke up. He said he lived a few blocks away and was grateful Jace had done what he could. "You did a lot," the older man said. "You pulled Melly from the fire and saved her baby. Anything I can help you with, you just say the word."

"Her name was Melly?"

"Melissa Smith." The landlord's eyes were wet now. "She always said to call her Melly."

Roxy started in again with the questions. Jace patiently answered everything she asked him.

Then it was his turn.

He gave the landlord a nod. "The baby's mother. Tell me more about her."

"Of course. Melly was a real sweetheart. Only nineteen and working two jobs to make ends meet. She was all on her own with that baby coming, and still, she always had a smile and a good word for everyone."

The landlord kept talking and Roxy recorded everything he said. From him, Jace learned that Melissa was subletting, and that her steady boyfriend, the baby's father, had died last year around Thanksgiving.

"Melly and her boyfriend, Kenny, grew up in the foster care system," the landlord said, and then he confirmed that what Melissa had told Jace was true. Neither of the baby's deceased parents had next of kin.

"Melly used to talk about being completely on her own." The landlord spoke solemnly. "She said that, yes, she'd lost the only boy she'd ever loved, but she always swore that her baby would grow up safe and happy, just like other kids. That they would be a family of two, Melly and her boy."

He thought of the things Melissa had shared with him as her baby was being born. "She mentioned a friend who was supposed to drive her to the hospital."

The landlord's wide brow wrinkled with a frown. "Yeah. Probably Alicia Simes. Barely eighteen. Skinny little thing. She and Melly worked together at that diner over on West Street. Alicia just graduated high school a few weeks ago."

So, then, Jace thought grimly, not a candidate to raise the baby.

When the landlord finally wound down and Roxy seemed to have no more questions, Jace brought up Morris.

"She loved that cat," said the landlord with a slow, regretful shake of his head.

"The cat ran out when I entered Melissa's apartment," Jace explained. "She was worried about him. Have you seen him by any chance?"

The landlord only shrugged. "Sorry, son—but I'll keep an eye out for him."

Jace took out his phone and they exchanged numbers. Then he turned to Roxy, described the cat and asked her if she would mention Morris in the *Bulletin*.

She promised she would. "You'll have that cat back in no time," she predicted.

The landlord started worrying out loud—about his tenants upstairs whose apartment was also gutted, about how soon the insurance company would cut him a check. Jace offered his hand and they shook.

Roxy said, "You take care now, Jace." And the landlord thanked him some more.

Wearily, Jace headed for the feed store. From there he went on to the station, where they pretty much had the cleanup under control. Chief Foster told him to go home and get himself some dinner.

He didn't argue. By then, he was moving on autopilot. He needed a shower, food and to zone out in front of his living room big screen.

At the Bonnie B, he drove past the main house and straight to his comfortable two-story cabin. The dogs ran out to greet him. Just the sight of them lightened the heavy weight that seemed to press on his heart.

Luna, a big, shaggy, beautiful Landseer New-foundland, fell right over on her back for a belly scratch. Bailey, a boxer/Great Pyrenees mix, dropped to her haunches politely, waiting her turn.

He'd just finished loving up both of them when his sister Robin came racing over from her house. "Jace!" She paused at the sight of him and looked him up and down. "Hard day, huh?"

He raked a hand back through his hair. "You could say that."

"You made the news again," she said. "And it's all over Facebook and Instagram, too—how you pulled that poor woman from the fire and delivered her baby." She made a low, sympathetic sound. "You look like you really need a hug."

He scoffed. "I appreciate the offer, but I'm covered in soot and other things you don't want to know about."

Robin was not put off. "Like I care."

Right then, they both heard the sound of an engine. His mom's Grand Cherokee came speeding toward them from the gravel road that led back to the main house.

Jerking to a stop, Bonnie Abernathy jumped out and strode right for him. "Come here." Before he could say a word, she grabbed him in a hug. Robin piled on. For a sweet little minute, he stood there between his mom and the older of his two sisters, glad to be an Abernathy with a big family to count on.

Then his mom took him by the shoulders. "I heard about the fire and that poor woman and her innocent newborn baby." She looked up at him through misty eyes. "I'm glad you were there." He hung his head at that—and she instructed, "Look at me, son." He lifted his head, and she said, "Am I your mama or not? I know you, Jace, if anyone does. You did all you could. Now, get a quick shower and join us at the main house for dinner."

"Mom, I need—"

She finished his sentence for him. "A good meal and your family around you. Now, get moving. The rib roast is coming out of the oven any minute now." She dipped her head at his sister. "Robin will be joining us for the evening meal, too, won't you?"

His sister gave a wry laugh. "Well, I guess I will now."

Twenty minutes later, he sat down with his family at the big dining room table in the log mansion where he'd been born. Everyone treated him gently—they knew how he got when a life was lost on his watch. He felt so lucky, to have them all, to know that no matter what, they all had each other's backs.

But who'd had Melly Smith's back? In the end, she was gone, with no family to step up and raise her baby boy.

"There's really no one at all?" his mom demanded.

"Doesn't look like it, Mom. Not from what Melissa Smith told me. And I stopped by her apartment building before I came home and talked to her landlord and Roxy James from the *Bulletin*. The landlord also seemed certain that neither Melissa nor the baby's father, who died last year, had any living relatives."

"I'll make some calls, find out what I can." His mom, who'd gotten her master's at UCLA, had been a social worker for years. Retired now, she still had a lot of connections in social services. Plus, she had a huge network of friends and the clout that being an Abernathy brought with it.

"I stopped in at the hospital to check on him," Jace said. "The nurse I talked to said Child and Family Services would be showing up soon."

"True," his mom confirmed. "In a case like this, usually within twenty-four to thirty-six hours."

His promise to Melissa nagged at him. If he didn't do something soon, the little boy would be put exactly where Melissa hadn't wanted him to be—in the system.

His mom suggested, "If nobody's taken care of it yet, we'll arrange for a simple memorial service for the mother—Saturday, most likely."

"That's fast."

"I'm pretty sure we can make it happen." She turned to Stacy, the youngest of the family, who taught at Bronco Elementary. "Help me out with this?"

Stacy didn't hesitate. "Of course, Mom."

Jace finished his dinner and even stuck around for coffee and pound cake. When he got up to go, there were more hugs and pats on the back.

Yeah, it was good to be surrounded by his family. But still, no way he could stop thinking about poor Melissa and that little boy who now had no family left.

In the predawn hours of the next morning, Jace mucked stalls and fed livestock with his dogs hanging out nearby.

Usually, he enjoyed early chores. Most of the time it was just him and the animals, everything calm and peaceful.

Too bad that today there was no peace for him.

The feeling of obligation nagged at him.

At eight in the morning, he called an auto body shop in town. Then he transferred all his gear from his crew cab to one of the ranch pickups.

He'd just gotten out of the shower at nine when a tow truck arrived. The driver hooked up the crew cab and towed it away to the best body shop in Bronco Heights, where they would change out the blood-stained back seat and fix everything up good as new.

Because a truck wasn't like a human being. If you

had the money, you could make any vehicle good as new.

As he watched his pickup roll away behind the tow truck, his phone rang in his hand. It was some fast talker from the local TV station. They wanted to interview him about his "heroism" yesterday.

"I'm sorry," he said sincerely, "but I really don't have anything to say." The guy on the other end kept talking. Jace let him wind down before saying no again.

After he hung up, he just stood there in the grassy space in front of his cabin with Bailey and Luna sitting at his feet. The dogs stared up at him the way they did when they weren't sure what he planned to do next and hoped there might be herding or stick-throwing involved.

He dropped to a crouch and gave them both some scratches and strokes. "Sorry, ladies. I need to head on over to the office right now."

They looked at him so sorrowfully that he ordered them up into the bed of the old blue pickup and drove them over to the main house and around to the office in back.

This time of day, he had the office to himself. He sat down at his dad's ancient PC and wrote up a Missing Cat flyer, complete with a photo he found online of a cat that looked like the one he'd seen fleeing Melissa's burning apartment yesterday. After printing up a hundred copies, he dropped the dogs off at his place and headed into town.

He parked down the street from Melissa's building and spent a couple of hours posting the flyers on every available pole and lamppost.

Back in the blue truck again, he drove to Bronco Valley Hospital. He went straight to reception and asked the same woman he'd talked to yesterday if Tamara Hanson was on duty.

The woman was a lot less wary today. Maybe because he was all cleaned up, or maybe she'd read about him in the *Bronco Bulletin*.

She gave him a big smile and said, "Let me just check." Once again, the woman bustled off through the door behind her desk and returned to tell him that Tamara would be right out.

And she was. The pretty nurse came toward him down the same hallway as yesterday, all that thick brown hair pinned up in a crown of braids like a princess in a Disney movie, a warm smile on her face. But those eyes of hers, they weren't smiling. Something was off.

"Jace. Hi."

He returned her smile. "I came to see the baby again."

"Ah," she replied—and smiled even wider.

"Okay, look," he said. "Just come out with it. What's wrong?"

Instead of answering his question, she took his

arm. Her touch was light. He didn't mind her hand on him, didn't mind it at all. Still. He wished she would just tell him what the hell was going on. "Talk to me, Tamara."

"Please. Just come on over here. Let's sit down, shall we?"

Maybe if he humored her, she'd get to the point. "Sure."

She led him to a chair. "I have the sweetest story to tell you," she said, pulling him down to sit beside her.

He played along. "A story?"

"Yes. It's about the baby."

"Okay..."

"So, we all felt protective of him, as we do with every baby in our care. But with him, well, that goes double, because he's lost his mom and has no other family that we know of. We all took extra time with him, holding him, talking to him, making sure he got that all-important human contact that newborns—and all children—need so much."

"That's great," he said, and wondered when she would finally cut to the chase. "Is he all right?"

"Oh, yeah. He's fine. Healthy. Doing well. Now, where was I? Oh, right. So. We didn't know at first that his mother's last name was Smith. We started calling him the Franklin baby, after the street he was born on. And then, well, we all decided that 'the Franklin baby' wasn't any kind of name for that sweet little guy. It was just natural, you know, to start calling him Frankie…" Her voice trailed off. She looked at him expectantly.

Before he could figure out what to say, she went right on. "So, anyway, by the time I left at seven yesterday evening, that baby was Frankie and that was that." Her smile glowed. Her eyes, not so much. "Frankie," she said again. "It's cute, don't you think?"

"Yeah." And he could read her like he'd known her forever. She was definitely easing up on the main point here—and much too slowly if you asked him. "Whatever it is, Tamara, just tell me now."

She winced. "Oh, Jace…"

"What? What's the matter? Just say it."

"Yes. All right. I'm afraid you can't see Frankie right now."

"Why not?"

"Jace, he isn't here. Child and Family Services came for him an hour ago. By now he's probably with a loving foster family." She started to put her hand over his.

He drew it back before she made contact. "But it hasn't even been twenty-four hours."

"What can I tell you? Sometimes these things happen fast."

"No kidding."

Now she looked at him pleadingly. "If no family is found for him, he will be adopted quickly. Healthy newborn babies always are. His new parents will want him and love him and be grateful every day that they were fortunate enough to become his mom and dad."

Jace, normally the calmest of men, jumped to his feet and accused far too loudly, "What the hell, Tamara? I told you I promised his mother that *I* would take care of him!"

The security guard left his post by the entrance and came running. Tamara, her back ramrod-straight now, gave the guard a quick shake of her Disney-princess head. The man stopped in his tracks. When she shook her head a second time, the guard gave it up and went back to his post.

She met Jace's eyes. Hers were steely now. "You need to keep it down," she said in a near whisper, every word clipped and crystal clear despite how quietly she was speaking. "If you don't, I can't help you. I *will* have the guard escort you out."

Jace dragged in a long breath and dropped to the chair again. He hung his head. Dear God, he hated this.

Was he even ready to take on the responsibility of a baby? Probably not. Did he *want* to be a dad? Someday, sure. But right now? The idea had never crossed his mind before yesterday.

But he had given Melissa his word. She'd died believing that he would follow through. He could not let her down. He just couldn't.

He made himself look directly into Tamara's

brown eyes. "I'm sorry." When she said nothing, he went on, "I don't know why I did that. You're trying to help and I'm taking my frustration out on you. It's just that I really feel responsible for that baby. I feel responsible, and I promised his mother I would raise him as my own, and somehow, I have to make that happen. I made a promise and I *have* to keep it."

Tamara felt her stiff spine loosen a fraction.

She might be a little put out in general with the male of the species lately—and for very good reason, too—but Jace Abernathy was not her ex. As cynical as she felt about men nowadays, even she could see that the one sitting beside her right now was a good guy who'd given his word to a dying mother, and just couldn't accept the fact that there was no way he would ever be able to keep his vow.

She glanced at her watch. "Listen…"

"Sorry." He drew his big body up straight in the chair. "I know you need to get back to work, and here I am keeping you from it." He was on his feet once more, towering over her, a ruggedly handsome man with sincerity shining in his green eyes. "Thank you."

Yep. A good guy. "Actually, Jace, that wasn't what I was going to say. I know you're upset that they took Frankie off before you could see him again."

He stood even taller and squared those thick shoulders. "I'll be okay."

She marveled at him a little. So straightforward and determined. He still didn't get that there was no way he was going to suddenly be allowed to raise that orphaned baby. And for some reason she didn't really even understand, she wanted to help him accept that baby Frankie would never call him Dad. "Listen, I'm going to take my lunch break now. Join me in the cafeteria? We can talk this through some more."

He stuck his hands in his pockets and studied his boots for a minute before slanting her a glance. "You think you can help me?"

She didn't want to lie, so she tried to find the right words to let him down easy. "Jace, I…"

He spoke into the silence between them. "The thing is, last year I made a promise I couldn't keep. I'm not letting that happen this time. One way or another, I *will* keep my promise to Melissa Smith." And then his mouth curved in a smile. "As for lunch, yes. And I'm buying."

Ten minutes later, she had a Greek salad and he had a club sandwich with fries. They took a two-seater table by a window that looked out on a small, landscaped courtyard.

"I'm curious," she said. "About that promise you made last year."

He picked up his sandwich, took a bite and stared out the window as he chewed and swallowed. When he faced her again, he shook his head. "I shouldn't have said that. It's not a happy story, and right now I really want to talk about Frankie."

Tamara kept her mouth shut. She waited.

And the man across from her caved. "Fine," he said bleakly. "I never should have brought up what happened last year. But I did. And if you really want to hear about it…"

"Yes, Jace. I do."

He stared out the window some more. She let the silence stretch out. Finally, he began. "Early last summer, I pulled an unconscious man from a burning ranch house southeast of town. My buddy brought out the man's ten-year-old son. I started CPR on the father. He regained consciousness, and the first thing he did was yank off the oxygen mask I'd put on him to ask me was where was his boy. I reassured him that the boy was in good hands. But the man was understandably freaked for his kid. He kept pulling off the mask, trying to get up. I couldn't settle him down.

"It became more of a battle than anything else. He struggled to get up. I held him down. He begged me to swear that his boy would be okay. I made the noises—as a nurse, you know what they are. That we were doing everything we could, that he needed to relax and let the oxygen help him. I did everything but give him the truth."

"And he wasn't having that?"

"No. Every time I'd get the mask back on, he

would rip it off. He was choking on his words, coughing so hard I wondered if he'd ever be able to stop. But he wouldn't give up. He kept struggling, fighting me, demanding that I promise him his son wouldn't die."

"So you promised him."

"Yeah. I swore that his boy would pull through— and you can probably guess what actually happened, right?"

She swallowed hard and gave a slow nod.

He said, "The kid died."

"Jace. It wasn't your—"

"Stop. I told that man a lie."

"You didn't know." She leaned toward him across the table, keeping her gaze locked with his, her voice low, urgent. "It turned out you were wrong, but that doesn't make it a lie. You said what you had to say so a desperate man would let you treat him."

"Yeah, well. Still a lie. After that broken promise, I swore to myself that I would never again deal in promises I can't keep."

"Sometimes it just happens that way. You know that. First responders do whatever it takes to save lives. And your job was to get that man to lie back down and let you help him."

"Make all the excuses you can think of for what I did. It doesn't change the hard fact that promises matter. I couldn't keep my promise to that dying boy's father. But my promise to Frankie's mother?

One way or another, I will find a way to do what I said I would do."

"Jace…"

He put up a hand between them. "I get it. Now you're going to tell me I shouldn't be so hard on myself, aren't you? You're going to try to get me to accept that I can't keep my promise to Melissa, either."

"Let's look at this from another angle."

He scowled at her. "What are you getting at?"

"Just think…."

He blew out a slow breath. "Think what?"

"Have you ever taken care of a baby? Do you have any idea of what a big job it is? That baby will need you round-the-clock. Right now, Frankie can't even hold his own head up—and don't imagine it's going to get easier. Uh-uh. Helping him grow up is going to be a full-time job, too."

"I know that."

"But, Jace, are you sure you're prepared to take on that kind of responsibility? Are you ready to be up all night when he gets colic or an earache? If you're honest with yourself, I think you will have to admit that you're simply not."

He looked at her steadily. "You don't know me." His voice was firm and calm, and his eyes didn't waver. "You don't know what I'm prepared for. I can learn to change a diaper and heat up formula—and I have a big family. Two brothers, two sisters. Two nephews and a niece who are all old enough to babysit now and then. My mom's retired and she will help out. I know she will. My dad, too, for that matter. It's all doable. I just need advice from you. I need you to tell me anything you might know about *how* to challenge the system so that I can keep my promise to Frankie's mother."

She took a long sip of iced coffee. When she put the glass down, she admitted, "You are very convincing. I believe you would do whatever it might take to keep your promise to Melissa Smith."

"You're right. I would—and I will."

"But, Jace, there's no way around the system. If no family can be found, Frankie will go to a couple who've done all they need to do to be eligible to adopt. You're starting from scratch here and you're single. Preference always goes to couples. And trying to foster him first and take it from there? As I said yesterday, getting qualified to be a foster parent takes time—three to six months, sometimes longer. Way before you can get certified as a foster parent, Frankie will be adopted and living with his new parents—loving parents who, right this minute, are waiting in line, ready to go, praying for a chance to bring home a newborn child like Frankie to raise as their own."

She could see it in his face. No matter what she said, he was not giving up.

"Sometimes impossible things can happen, Tamara."

"True. But probably not *this* impossible thing."

He only gazed at her steadily, no more convinced that he needed to give this up than he'd been twenty minutes ago, back there in the waiting area.

They finished their lunch in silence.

Then he said, "Just play along with me here for a minute. Just say the impossible happens and I do get to bring Frankie home…" She opened her mouth to remind him—again—that he needed to be realistic about this. But before she could get a word out, he said, "Hold on. Just humor me. You work with the babies here, right?"

"Yes. And with the moms. I'm a maternal/child nurse, though I also help out wherever I'm needed. It's a small hospital, after all."

"If I did get to take care of Frankie, I would really like to be able to reach out to you, to ask you all the questions I don't even know I'm going to need the answers to yet."

"But you won't—"

"Yeah, but if I did, would you help me, Tamara?"

She wavered. His green eyes were full of hope and sincerity and…

Well, the truth was, she liked the guy. Right now, her natural tendency was to distrust the majority of men on principle. Yet somehow, his frankness and honesty had broken right through her considerable defenses.

If the impossible did happen somehow, of course she would help him.

For Frankie's sake.

"All right, Jace. If you actually managed to take the baby home, I would be happy to help you any way I could."

He grinned that warm and charming grin of his—and whipped out his phone. "Give me your number."

She blinked and sat back in her chair. Was he making a move on her?

No. Of course not.

Still, it would be best to make things very clear right up front. After the disaster with Eric, she was taking an open-ended break from anything remotely resembling romance. "Jace, I…"

His brow wrinkled with a puzzled sort of frown. "What's wrong?"

"Well…" She coughed nervously. "Just to be clear, I'm not looking for a date, or anything."

He gave her a teasing grin. "Tamara, don't tempt me."

That made her smile. "Okay, then. But just so we're on the same page about this."

"We are. I get your number, but only for Frankie's sake."

"That's right." She rattled it off. A moment later, her phone buzzed with a text.

"And now you have mine," he said.

By then, they'd both finished lunch. She walked

him out to reception, wished him well and watched him walk away—head high, shoulders straight, as sure as he'd ever been that one way or another, he would end up raising that orphaned little boy.

Thinking how much she liked him, almost feeling sad that she would probably never hear from him again, she turned back toward the hallway that led to the nurses' station. She was so busy feeling weirdly wistful over Jace Abernathy that she didn't realize Dr. Eric Pearce was walking right toward her until he was practically on top of her.

"Tamara," he said with a nod and that knowing smirk of his, the one she used to think was so magnetic and sexy.

"Dr. Pearce." She gave him a brisk nod and kept on walking. Ugh. It was the only really bad part of her job, having to see Eric all the time—Eric and that blonde backstabber, Elise Wayne, the anesthesiologist he'd cheated on her with.

He and Elise were together now. More power to them. They deserved each other.

And she wasn't spending one more second of her day thinking about them. She had plenty of work to do and she loved her job.

Hours later, Tamara came through the door from the NICU to find her friend and fellow nurse Stephanie Brandt waiting for her.

"You have to see this." Stephanie grabbed her hand and started pulling her up the hallway.

"What's going on?" Tamara held back.

"You'll see." Even in the glare of the too-bright hospital lighting, Stephanie was gorgeous, her brown skin nothing short of luminous. "Come on."

With a groan, Tamara allowed her friend to drag her along.

Stephanie slowed at the door to the staff lounge and pushed it open. "This way."

Inside, half the staff had congregated around the flatscreen mounted on the wall above the big round break table.

"What the...?" Tamara blinked in disbelief at what she saw on that screen.

It was Jace on the local TV station, KBTV. He'd changed his clothes since lunch. Now he wore a crisp cobalt blue button-down and a handsome Western jacket. His face was freshly shaved, his thick brown hair combed neatly back. He sat at a table with Odell White, the host of the local news show.

"That's right," Jace said. "I was able to bring Melissa Smith safely out of her burning apartment. She was far along in labor at that point and ended up having her baby in the back seat of my truck."

The host looked appropriately somber. "But I understand that the mother didn't make it."

"Sadly, no."

"And the baby?"

"He's doing well. Right now, he's in foster care." Jace let that sink in a moment before going on to share the promise he'd made to Frankie's mom. "Melissa Smith told me that she has no next of kin. And that neither did Frankie's father, who died last fall. It was Melissa's last wish that I raise her little boy. I promised her I would."

"Frankie?" Odell White asked. "That's the baby's name?"

"It's what the staff at Bronco Valley Hospital started calling him." Jace launched right into the story Tamara had told him of how Frankie got his name.

"He looks good," whispered Stephanie. "So convincing."

Tamara had to agree. He looked better than good, calm and collected, in command of himself, sure of what was right.

No, social services would not throw out all their rules so that he could keep his promise to Frankie's lost mother. The world didn't work that way.

But right now, for the first time, Tamara found herself thinking that it was too bad, really. Because little Frankie Smith could do worse than to be raised by a man like Jace Abernathy.

Chapter Three

Dinner, Tamara thought wearily as she drove home early that evening. She needed to decide about that. Either she would eat out again, pick something up at a drive-through or stop at the grocery store.

With a sigh, she chose the healthiest option, pulling in at the big supermarket on Commercial Street to grab some chicken to cook and a bag of salad. She ought to do some real shopping soon, because at home, the cupboards were bare.

She found a parking space right away and ran in, heading for the meat department, grabbing a package of chicken thighs, moving on to produce and then realizing she was out of coffee and a few other things. With a sigh, she rolled her cart up and down the aisles, tossing in the stuff she needed as she went.

In the bread aisle, as she vacillated between whole wheat and sourdough, she happened to glance over—and there was Jace.

He wore what he'd worn for his interview that afternoon, minus the jacket. The blue button-down, as it turned out, was short sleeved. It showed off the strong muscles of his powerful forearms. He looked way too hot and hunky as he read the label on a jar of jam.

Of course, he turned his head and spotted her. "Tamara, hey!" He looked really happy to see her, and that made her feel just a little bit giddy.

Uh-uh. Nope.

Okay, he seemed like a good person, but so had Eric and look how that had turned out. She simply couldn't trust her own judgment, not about men.

Jace came on like a regular guy. He seemed thoughtful, polite and respectful. But he was an Abernathy, and the Abernathys had both money and power.

He'd probably pulled strings to get himself that interview today, used his last name to get on TV and tell the whole town that he should be the one to adopt an orphaned baby, when there were couples who had jumped through all the hoops already and now were waiting their turn, praying for their chance to raise a little boy like Frankie.

Those hopeful couples mattered. Jace Abernathy had no right to cut in front of them.

And she was not getting all worked up over any man, not even one as appealing as Jace. Not tonight—not for a long time.

"Hey!" She gave him a quick, cool nod, grabbed the nearest loaf of bread and speed walked in the other direction.

At the checkout counter, she kept her head down. She was out the wide glass doors in no time. Too bad that when she got back to her RAV4, she discovered that her left rear tire had gone flat.

"Terrific," she muttered.

Resigned, she put the groceries in the back seat. Then she went to work, freeing her spare tire, car jack, lug wrench, wheel wedges, portable tire pump and tire gauge from beneath the rear floor mat.

She was crouched by the flat tire, positioning the jack, when a pair of high-dollar boots came into view and a now-familiar deep voice said, "Hold on. I'll put these bags in my truck and take care of that for you."

She looked up—way up—to see Jace smiling down at her from between his own two full grocery bags. "Thanks, but I've got this. You go on. I really do know how to change a tire."

"Fair enough." He turned and walked away.

Which was good, excellent. He'd done exactly what she'd told him to do and that suited her just fine.

Not two minutes later, he was back, minus the groceries, carrying the one thing she didn't have—a kneeling pad. "I see you've got pretty much everything you need," he said.

"Yes, I do."

"But this might help." He held out the pad.

Fine. A kneeling pad *would* help. She hadn't been looking forward to dirtying up the knees of her scrubs.

He dipped to a crouch and set down the pad.

All she could say was, "Thank you, Jace."

He backed off, but he didn't leave—which made sense. He was waiting for her to finish with the pad. Once she got the car up on the jack and started removing the lug nuts, he came forward. "I'll just hold those for you until you're ready for them again."

After that, she started to feel foolish, being so cool and distant with him, judging him so harshly when he was only trying to help. They ended up working together. It went a lot faster with all that upper body strength he had.

When they finished and the tools and flat tire were put away, she shared her tub of wipes with him, though he said he had his own.

"Come on," she coaxed. "I really appreciate the use of your kneeling pad and your help, too. The least you can do is take a couple of my wipes."

"Well, when you put it that way..." He cleaned his big hands and suggested, "Join me for a burger at Doug's?"

As she dithered over whether or not to say yes,

he said, "This afternoon, I went on KBTV. They interviewed me live—about Frankie."

"I saw that, yeah." She might have left it at that, but he was looking at her so hopefully, like her opinion of his on-air performance really mattered to him. "You did great."

He let out a slow breath. "I hope so. When I left the station, I wasn't sure. I drove all the way home, got my dogs and went out and sat by the creek that runs through a pretty little canyon a couple miles from my cabin. I was feeling all jittery and hopped up from the tension of being on TV."

"You were? You seemed so calm during the interview."

"I *was* calm while it was happening. I'm always that way in a crisis. It's afterward that I worry and wonder, second-guessing, trying to push away the feeling that I've blown it somehow.

"Anyway, I sat there by the creek thinking about all the things I should have said until I remembered that I'd been obsessing so hard over that interview I forgot to get groceries. So I dropped the dogs off at the cabin and drove back into town."

They stared at each other. It was no hardship, staring at Jace.

As for his invitation, why not? It was only a burger, after all. "I need to stop by my house. Put the perishables in the fridge."

He seemed puzzled. "Was that a yes?"

"Yes, it was. I'll meet you at Doug's, my treat."

He frowned. And then he gave her a slow smile. "You want to buy me a burger?"

"And a beer, too. In appreciation."

"For...?"

"The use of your kneeling pad and the thoughtful way you stepped up to hold my lug nuts."

For yet another almost-electric moment, they just looked at each other some more. Then they both laughed. "Fair enough." He lifted his big arm, his powerful biceps and forearm muscles flexing, the prominent veins popping into higher relief as he rubbed the back of his neck. She couldn't help thinking that arm porn might be a real thing, after all. "Half an hour, then," he said.

Reminding herself sternly that ogling a man was rude—and kind of sexist, to boot—she replied, "See you at Doug's."

At her cute little two-bedroom cottage a few blocks from Commercial Street, Tamara stuck the chicken and produce in the fridge and then headed for her bedroom to change out of her scrubs. She was two steps down her short hallway when she stopped herself.

Because what was her problem? This was a burger between friends and nothing more. Burgers between friends did not require a change of clothes or a detour to the bathroom to freshen her makeup and let down her hair.

"Rreeow?"

She turned to find her cat, Harley, peering at her from the front end of the hall. "Hey, baby."

He strutted toward her.

Scooping him up, she buried her nose in his sleek black fur. "How've you been all day?" Harley rubbed his cheek against hers and purred even louder. "I'll bet you want your dinner."

For that he gave her a low, throaty growl, so she carried him back to the kitchen, opened him a can of cat food and refilled his water bowl before she headed out the door.

At Doug's, a friendly server led her to a small table across the restaurant from the long bar.

Jace was already there. He jumped up and held her chair before she could tell him not to.

"Thanks."

"My pleasure." He returned to his chair and the server took their order.

Doug came over to chat a little as they waited for the food. So did a couple of women and a tall, thin guy in faded jeans and a flannel shirt. They'd seen Jace's interview and wanted to tell him that they were rooting for him to get custody of Frankie.

He thanked them.

When they were alone again, Tamara asked, "So

how did you end up convincing KBTV to give you a segment?"

He hitched one powerful shoulder in a half shrug. "I didn't."

"Wait. *They* called *you*?"

He nodded. "They called me this morning to ask me to come on the afternoon news and talk about the fire. I said no at that time."

That surprised her. "Why?"

"Just feeling low, thinking about Melissa Smith. She seemed like a really sweet girl, and now she's gone. I only spent a short amount of time with her, but it was so obvious how much she loved her baby, how much she wanted him to have what she never had when she was growing up. I was feeling pretty low when the station called me, and I just wasn't in the mood to talk about what happened."

"What changed your mind?"

The server came back with their draft beers.

As soon as she left, Jace picked up his mug and drank. "To be honest with you," he said as he set the mug down, "I changed my mind after you told me all the reasons there was no way I would ever become Frankie's dad. As soon as I left the hospital, I called the station back. They were only too happy to put me on the afternoon news."

Guilt prodded at her. Had she been too hard on him earlier?

No. She really hadn't. She'd been gentle. She'd only tried to get him to face facts.

Jace said, "I know what you think, Tamara. You've made it painfully clear. But I figure it can't hurt to put myself out there, to let the whole town know that Melissa Smith wanted *me* to take care of Frankie." His eyes shone with sheer determination. He seemed absolutely set on doing what he thought was right.

Her carefully constructed defenses against him— against men in general lately—crumbled just a little. She really needed to stop judging the guy and admit the truth about him.

Jace Abernathy was a fine man, responsible and caring. When he looked at her with all that fire in his eyes, she believed that he was one hundred percent sincere in his certainty that he should be the one Frankie called Dad.

Still, he really did need to be realistic. "Listen, Jace…"

He scoffed, but gently. "Here's the part where you tell me—again—that what I want is impossible, right?"

"I just hate to see you get your hopes up, that's all. You're a single man with zero child-rearing experience. You couldn't pass a home study—I'm guessing you don't even know what a home study is."

"Yes, I do. It's an evaluation of a person's fitness for the job of adopting a child or fostering one, the screening process you mentioned yesterday, the one you said can take several months. You see, my mom's a retired social worker. I'm going to ask her to help me speed the process up."

Well. The man really was full of surprises. "I didn't know that about your mom."

"Yeah. The truth is, she's got connections and clout, and I'm going to take shameless advantage of all that. Because doing what Melissa begged me to do—that's the *right* thing to do."

"Oh, Jace…"

He leaned in, eyes gleaming even brighter than before. "Don't underestimate me, Tamara. Generally, I'm pretty easygoing. But when I really set my mind on something, watch out."

The server chose that moment to bring them their burgers. When she left them, Tamara said, "I believe you. I know you're sincere about this. But, Jace, it's just not going to happen."

He gave her a slow, careful nod. "You've got a right to your opinion. But I think you're wrong. I have a really good feeling about this."

What could she say to that except, "So, then I guess we agree to disagree."

He let a half shrug and a rueful smile be his answer. Then he asked, "You're not from town, are you?"

She teased, "Are we changing the subject?"

"Yes, we are. So tell me, Tamara, where did you grow up?"

"I was born in Santa Barbara."

"But you didn't grow up there?"

"My mom and dad divorced when I was five."

"And then what?"

She ate a french fry. "You really want to know?"

"I wouldn't ask if I didn't."

"All right, then. After my parents divorced, my mom and I moved to Los Angeles. From then on, I didn't see much of my birth father. I grew up with my mom and a series of stepdads. We moved a lot. From LA we went to Phoenix. Then to Austin. My mom lives in Palm Springs now with her fourth husband."

"Brothers and sisters?"

"Nope. You'd have to know my mom. She's kind of high-maintenance. She's always said that one child was way more than enough. So yeah, I would have loved to have a little sister or a brother, but that's not how it worked out."

"What brought you to Bronco?"

"Five years ago I answered an ad for an RN with maternal/child experience at Bronco Valley Hospital. I got the job, so here I am." She'd always wanted a settled-down life, doing meaningful work with a good man at her side and kids of her own. Until a little while ago, she'd thought she'd found that man in Eric. Wrong. "I love it here. Small-town life agrees with me."

"Ever been married?"

"Nope." And she'd definitely answered enough questions for now. "What about you, Jace?"

"I haven't been married, no."

"Do you want to get married someday?"

His nod was firm. "I do, yeah. As soon as I find the right girl."

She almost asked what kind of woman he was looking for exactly.

But come on. Really? Why were they talking about marriage?

Yeah, he'd brought up the subject. But then she'd turned right around and started in on him about it. It wasn't like they were dating or anything. They didn't need to reassure each other that they were on the same page with their, er, romantic life goals.

The server returned. Jace said he would love one more beer. And Tamara went ahead and said she'd have one, too.

When they were alone again, she asked about his family. He told her about his brothers. About Billy, the oldest, who rode the rodeos when he was younger. About second-born Theo, who had a podcast called *This Ranching Life*. When she asked about his sisters, he proudly announced that Robin had created her own line of horse therapeutics, and Stacy, the youngest, taught elementary school.

"My mom and dad are still going strong in their sixties," he said. "They both work the family ranch along with the rest of us—meaning they are in great shape, always willing to help out. Right now they have three grandchildren, and they're always hoping for more—so as you can see, I have an excellent support system to pitch in taking care of Frankie." He winked.

She made a show of rolling her eyes. "Just had to get that in there, didn't you?"

"Pretty smooth, huh?"

"And persistent."

"I try."

"Oh, Jace. I would say you do a lot more than just *try*."

The server returned with their beers. They sipped them slowly, talking and laughing together. She probably should have cut the evening short. But she was having a really good time.

It was dark when they left the bar, the night sky cloudless and thick with stars. "It's another thing I love about Montana," she said. "Some nights the stars seem close enough to reach up and touch."

A couple of cowboys got out of a battered pickup. Jace greeted them by name.

"You know everyone in this town?" she asked.

He shrugged. "Sometimes it feels that way."

They reached her little SUV, and she beeped the locks. Jace pulled her door open for her.

She got in. "Thanks," she said.

He chuckled. "For what? You picked up the tab."

"And I was more than happy to pay the check. You're good company, Jace Abernathy."

He tipped his hat at her. "Well, I had a real good time, too. Drive safe."

"I will."

He shut the door and stepped back, but then just stood there. A glance in her rearview mirror had her thinking how alone he looked, so tall and strong and serious, watching her as she drove away.

At home, Jace paid some attention to Bailey and Luna and then went to bed. He was feeling jazzed after spending the evening with Tamara. She was the kind of woman who kept a man on his toes.

He laced his hands behind his head and stared up at the shadowed bedroom ceiling, thinking about the things she'd said. She remained so certain that he would never be the one to raise Frankie.

She was wrong about that. He just knew that things would work out. Grinning, he closed his eyes.

When he opened them again, it was a little after four in the morning. He got up, had some coffee and headed for the barns.

Later, as he and his brothers moved cattle to fresh pastures, his thoughts kept circling back to Tamara. The woman was as capable as they came. She wouldn't even let him change her tire. And he'd liked that she wouldn't. He'd liked it a lot.

He liked looking at her, too—so much grit and

can-do spirit in such a small, fine-looking package. Last night at Doug's, he couldn't keep his mind from going sexy places. He'd imagined helping her take down her crown of braids. He'd pictured himself peeling off those baby blue scrubs of hers, getting an eyeful of the curves underneath.

Would she have taken offense if she'd known what he was thinking, as she talked about her mom and her stepdads and being an only child, as she quizzed him about whether or not he ever intended to get married?

Probably.

He grinned even wider. Because Tamara Hanson was nothing like the women he usually got involved with. Tamara didn't need his help with anything. She ran her own life and from what he could see, she did a fine job of it—and still, Jace was very much attracted to her. For the first time, he wanted a woman who didn't need a man to take care of her. He was downright proud of himself for getting to that point.

The last couple of years, he'd done some serious thinking about his compulsion to come to the rescue of anyone in need. For a long time now, he'd known what his problem was. He'd taken a few elective psychology classes while getting his degree at Montana State. What he had was called white knight syndrome, and it had really messed with his love life from all the way back to his first girlfriend, Genevra Lang, when he was fourteen.

When he and Genevra had gotten together, her

mom had recently died. Jace couldn't help but notice that Genny constantly battled tears during Latin class, so he'd made it a point to befriend her.

Friendship with Genny had turned romantic fairly quickly. Soon enough, she was always at his side—to the point that she didn't seem to want him to do anything else but be with her. They broke up junior year. After the homecoming game in which he scored the winning touchdown, she demanded that he choose—football, firefighting and 4H—or her.

It had taken him a while to admit it to himself, but by the holidays, he'd realized that it was never going to work with her.

So he'd moved on from Genevra, but he hadn't changed. He'd kept right on choosing the sad girls, the ones who looked lonely or desperate—the ones in serious need of a friend. He'd felt driven to help them get through whatever tough time they were having.

Inevitably, helping would turn into something more intimate. But somehow, just like with Genny, those relationships always ended unhappily. He would begin to wish for someone more self-sufficient—and his girlfriends would grow frustrated and angry that he'd pulled back, stopped giving them the constant reassurance and attention they craved and needed.

But Tamara Hanson didn't need anyone to rescue her. She could rescue herself just fine. The woman had almost as many useful tools in her little SUV as he had in his pickup, proving she was ready at any time to deal with a wide range of emergencies. After knowing her only a short time, he had zero doubt that she would always try hard to solve her own problems.

Later that afternoon, he and Luna and Bailey got back to his cabin to find his mom sitting on the front porch. The two dogs, crowded into the small cab of the ranch truck with him, whined in eagerness at the sight of her.

When he opened the door and gave them permission to get down, his mom rose from the porch chair, arms outstretched as they ran to greet her. "Hey, girls. Come to Grandma." She knelt to hug and pet them, rising with the easy grace of a much younger woman as he mounted the steps. "How about a nice, tall glass of iced tea?" she offered.

He would have preferred a cold brew, but she'd brought a pitcher of tea over with her from the main house. It was right there on the round wooden table between the two Adirondack chairs. "That'd be great, Mom. Just give me five minutes to wash off a little of the day's grime."

"I'll wait out here with the ladies. Bring two glasses."

"Will do."

When he came back out, he handed her the glasses and took the empty chair.

She poured the iced tea, picked up her glass and raised it in a toast."Here's to you and your viral video." He must have looked as puzzled as he felt because she added, "Your TV interview yesterday ended up on YouTube and Facebook and just about everywhere else a person might put up a video. Now the world loves you. Everyone thinks you ought to be the one to raise that little baby you rescued."

It was a lot to take in. "They do?"

"Yes, they do."

"That's good, right?"

She set down her tea. "It's what you want, isn't it?"

"Yeah, Mom. It is."

"Well, it's not a done deal yet, but I've been fielding calls from my former colleagues at social services for most of the day."

"Calls about me and Frankie?"

"Yes. Child and Family Services has been inundated with phone messages and emails. The whole state of Montana thinks that you should get that baby boy. It's a PR nightmare for the agency."

"Wait. Is that bad?"

"Not for you, son. It all works in your favor—if you're really certain you *want* to be a dad, that is."

"I am, Mom. I'm absolutely sure."

She slanted him a skeptical glance. "It's that promise you made to his mother, isn't it? You feel driven to keep your word to her."

"I do, yeah."

"You can't rescue everyone, Jace."

Annoyance tightened his gut. "You think I don't know that by now?"

His mother narrowed her eyes at him. "Don't get snippy with me, young man. I'm here to help."

Now he felt like a jerk. "I'm sorry, Mom. You're right. I can't rescue everyone, and I really am learning to live with that. But I want to do this, for me. I've always wanted to be a family man eventually. And the more I think about it, the more I see that *eventually* is finally here. Because now there's Frankie. I want to help him grow up. I want to be a real dad to him."

"I see," said his mother. And then she smiled. "Well, all right, then. I want you to be a real dad, too."

"So you *are* going to help me?"

"Yes."

He breathed a sigh of relief. "Great. Because I need you on my side for this."

"I'm glad you realize that."

"I do, Mom. I see the whole picture. You live a short walk from my front door, you've raised five children and have thirty years' experience working in the system. It counts for a lot that you'll be nearby to make sure Frankie is properly taken care of."

"That's right." She reached across the table and fondly patted his hand. "You always were perceptive, Jace. And sensitive."

He didn't know what to say to that. "Just don't go

telling that to Billy and Theo. They already think I'm too soft for my own damn good."

"I will not say a word."

"Thanks, Mom." He felt kind of humbled. "And here I'd been thinking I would have to convince you to help me find a way to get custody of Frankie. Instead, you're already on board. I can't tell you how much your help means to me."

Her smile flattened out. "Let's not get ahead of ourselves, though."

From her tone and the stern look on her face, Jace knew that a lecture was forthcoming. He resigned himself to it. "It's okay, Mom. Say what you need to say."

"Oh, yes I will." She poured herself more tea and gave Bailey a scratch between the ears. "You know I love you and I think the world of you, son. But honestly, I can't help but wonder why you won't just find a nice girl and take it from there? You know how you are, with all those poor women you try to save. That never goes well, does it? And now this…"

"Mom, I—"

"However." She raised a hand as she cut him off. "It's true that you are a good man, a son I'm proud of. I understand that you made a promise, and I believe that you *want* to be a father to that child. But as your mother, I just can't pass up this opportunity to point out that, like your brothers before you, you have yet to establish a stable, healthy relationship with a woman who can be a true life partner to you."

She was really rolling now. "Honestly, I don't understand how all three of you are still single—and your sisters, too, for that matter. It's worrisome. It has your father and me wondering if we did something wrong, if the model of married life we provided for you was lacking somehow."

"Mom, no. You and Dad are not the problem. We all know that you love him and he worships the ground you walk on."

"Well, then what has gone wrong?" she demanded. And then before he could come up with a credible answer, she waved a hand. "Never mind. What I'm trying to say is, I'm hoping that this situation with Frankie will really get you thinking about the future. You need a good woman in your life. And if you do adopt that baby, he's going to need a mother."

Jace drank his tea and kept his mouth shut. Nodding, trying to look appropriately chastened and sincere, he listened to his mom's well-meaning rant—and thought about Tamara.

Because wouldn't his folks be surprised if he brought Tamara home? The petite nurse was so strong and capable. She didn't need any man to lean on. He grinned to himself just thinking about her.

"What *are* you grinning about, Jacey?" His mom used her baby name for him, the one she'd called him back when he couldn't button his own shirt. She did that when she thought he might not be paying attention to whatever wisdom she thought she was sharing.

And as for Tamara, well, she was amazing and he wanted to know her better. But he'd only just met her, really. He probably shouldn't let himself get too carried away too fast when it came to her.

"Jace." His mom sounded more than a little annoyed now. "Did you hear a word I just said?"

"Of course, I heard every word you said. I'm just, uh, really happy you're going to help me out with this."

"Yes, well…" She gave him a prim little smile and a nod to match. "You're welcome. And we have work to do, you and me. You will be assessed and screened, and all of that will be fast-tracked. You will need to pass an expedited home study. Bottom line, if you do everything I instruct you to do, you will be Frankie's foster dad within the next couple of weeks."

"But will that be fast enough? What if he gets adopted by someone else before then?"

His mother gave him her most patient, long-suffering look. "Your interview at KBTV yesterday took care of that. No one at the agency wants an avalanche of bad PR. No one else is going to suddenly adopt him. The baby will remain in his current foster home long enough for you to prove that you're up to the job of taking care of him. And given that Melissa and the baby's father both grew up in the system because neither of them had any family to care for them, some lost family member popping up out of nowhere is highly unlikely. All the *i*'s will be dotted and every *t* crossed, of course. But it's doubtful that some missing relative is going to suddenly step forward to sue for custody."

"You're sure, Mom?"

"Nothing is a given, Jace. But from what my former colleagues have shared with me, chances are excellent you can become Frankie's foster father and then go for adoption from there."

Jace felt humbled. His mom could talk the ears off a mule, but she backed up the talk with action. She was always right there, ready to help, any time he or his siblings needed her. "Wow. That's great, Mom. Terrific."

"We're going to have to put together a decent nursery in one of your bedrooms. And we'll need to figure out who in the family can help out with the baby and when. We might have to hire a nanny."

"Whatever needs doing, I'm ready for it."

She set down her tea and sat back with a happy sigh. "A new grandbaby." Now she was beaming again. "I'm so excited about this—and Jace, there is just so much to do!"

Chapter Four

When his mom finally left, Jace fed his dogs, ate a couple of sandwiches and had a shower—and then texted Tamara to share his good news.

Hey. Got a minute? We need to talk.

A moment later, the phone rang in his hand. When he put it to his ear, Tamara said in a careful tone, "Hello, Jace."

He teased, "Glad to hear from me at last after all this time?"

She gave the cutest little snicker and then demanded, "What's up?"

"Remember I told you my mom used to work for social services?"

"Yeah…"

"Well, she's been on the case."

"Meaning…?"

"She's been in constant contact all day today with her old friends at Child and Family Services. As of now, it looks like things might be going my way." He quickly recapped all his mom had laid out for him an hour before.

When he finished, Tamara was silent.

"Tamara? You still with me?"

"Yeah. I just… Wow."

"I know, right?"

"Your mom sounds like a force of nature."

"She's a powerhouse, no doubt about that. When she gets behind a project, things happen fast. And according to her, two weeks from now I will be a foster dad."

"Wow—sorry, I'm repeating myself."

"I understand, believe me."

"And I'm assuming you're still planning to adopt Frankie permanently?"

"That's right. My goal is to adopt Frankie. For now, though, I'm focused on getting approved to be a foster parent. To make that happen, I have a lot of work to do in a short period of time. And that's why I'm hoping you meant what you said about helping me get things ready for Frankie if I managed to find a way to be the one to take care of him."

She was quiet again.

He tried not to feel disappointed. "So...that's a no?"

She groaned. It was actually a very sexy sound. Or maybe that was just his dirty mind. "No, Jace. That is *not* a no. I said I would help and I will."

He should probably let her off the hook. She'd already said she wouldn't go out with him. Her current reluctance to help him with Frankie should be enough to make him take the hint and walk away.

But it wasn't. "Can we start tomorrow?"

Tamara hesitated, as she'd been doing throughout this surprising conversation.

It wasn't that she didn't want to help Jace. She did. Maybe too much.

Since last night, she'd been thinking about the handsome firefighting cowboy a lot. About his sweetness as a human being. About the way he seemed to want to do the right thing for its own sake. She really was beginning to believe that none of it was an act.

And that had her reconsidering her stance on his push to adopt Frankie. It had her realizing that yes, there were childless couples already approved to adopt, couples waiting for their chance to bring up a baby like Frankie. But Frankie's mother had chosen Jace, and her dying wish did matter, after all.

Or was Tamara only having all these second thoughts about him because she found him attractive? Because he had those big, strong arms and broad shoulders and that slow smile that made her wonder what kissing him would feel like?

"Tamara? You still there?"

"Uh, yes. Right here."

"Are you working tomorrow?"

"No. I'm off tomorrow." Sheesh. Had she given that up fast, or what?

"My mom's already set me up with an appointment to meet my caseworker at Child and Family Services tomorrow, and then I have my first group meeting with other future foster parents. Those will be ongoing as I get my foster-parent training. After the group meeting, I need to start getting my place in shape, shopping for a crib and all the baby stuff Frankie's going to need. And that's where you come in, if you're still willing."

"You want me to go shopping with you?" Had she just volunteered? Was that wise? Not in the least.

"Yes, I do." She could hear the smile in his deep, manly voice. "Say, four o'clock?"

She really should take a minute, think it over. But she didn't. "Four o'clock works for me."

"Give me your address. I'll pick you up."

She rattled the information off without the least hesitation.

When she hung up, she tossed her phone on the coffee table and called herself all kinds of foolish and ridiculous. Because she was way too attracted to Jace Abernathy, and she really wasn't sure she could help him without falling for him.

She felt something soft brushing her ankles—Harley, purring like a motorboat. Scooping him up, she nuzzled the ruff of his neck.

"Am I a fool, Harley? Just tell me."

Harley only purred louder.

Friday afternoon, Jace showed up right on time.

Tamara went to let him in with Harley at her heels. She should have watched the crafty cat more closely, but she was too busy thinking about the man on the other side of the door. Harley slipped through when she opened it.

"Whoa, big guy." Jace dipped to a crouch and scooped him up. "You let him outside?"

"Not if I can help it."

"He's purring." Jace smiled and then said to the cat, "You're a friendly one." He scratched Harley's head and the cat purred louder.

"He's not usually a big fan of strangers," she said. Wouldn't you know he'd choose Jace to adore on sight?

She watched Jace's big hand as he stroked Harley from forehead to the tip of his long sleek black tail. Harley closed his eyes and kept on purring.

"Seems pretty friendly to me." Jace looked up at her again, his brow furrowed now.

She asked, "What's the matter?"

He shook his head and went on petting Harley. "This guy has me thinking of Morris."

"That's Melissa Smith's cat, right?"

"Yeah. I put flyers all over her neighborhood with my number on them. Nobody's called."

"He'll turn up."

"I hope so."

She held out her arms and he passed Harley to her. She kissed him between his pointy black ears, backed out of the doorway and set him inside before pulling the door quickly shut.

They walked down the front steps side by side. "Nice truck," she said as he pulled open the front passenger door for her. She started to step up to the seat, but something stopped her. She turned and met his eyes. They were sadder than before, kind of haunted looking. "Oh, no. What did I say now?"

"Nothing you shouldn't have. It's just that the night we went to Doug's, I was driving one of the ranch trucks because this one was in the body shop. It needed new seats in back, among other things."

It took her a minute, but she put it together. "You delivered Frankie back there?"

He nodded. "I, uh, got lucky. The shop had the seats I needed."

She had no idea what to say. But she did want to ease his mind somehow. Before she could think better of it, she put her hand against his cheek, feeling the warmth of his skin and the slight scratch of beard shadow. "I'm so sorry," she heard herself whisper. "For Melissa. For Frankie. For all of it."

He nodded. And for another long moment, they simply stood there, staring into each other's eyes.

When he spoke, his voice was low, gentle, and yet also somehow torn around the edges. "Get on up in the truck."

She climbed into the passenger seat.

They shopped until after eight. When they finally called it a night, the back seat of his crew cab was packed with baby things. He had a shell on the truck bed. It was pretty full back there, too.

They were headed to her house when he announced, "I'm not taking you home until I've fed you. That wouldn't be right."

She tried to refuse—probably not as hard as she should have.

They ended up at a cozy Italian place in Bronco Valley. He mentioned the memorial service for Melissa tomorrow at two in the afternoon, at that little white church near Bronco Park.

"I heard," she said. "News spreads fast in Bronco."

"Are you going?"

She was off work again tomorrow. "Yeah, I'll be there."

He held her gaze, one corner of his mouth quirking up. "I'll pick you up."

She really wanted to say yes. But the whole point was not to get too wrapped up in this man—in any man. The point was to be enough on her own, not to need some guy to make her life complete.

"Thanks," she said, "but I've got errands to run before and after, so I'll drive my own car."

The next day, the church was full to overflowing. People stood in the aisles and on the steps outside the wide-open church doors.

Tamara had arrived early enough to get a seat in one of the back pews. As she waited for the service to begin, she thought how much she loved living in Bronco, how great it was that so many people had turned out for the memorial service of a woman most of them had never met.

But they'd all heard of Melissa Smith by now, from the story in the *Bronco Bulletin* and from Jace's interview on KBTV. They'd heard about her death and her orphaned baby, and they cared enough to come and pay their final respects.

The service was brief. The minister, a kind-faced middle-aged woman, talked about peace and love everlasting. She announced that Melissa had been buried the day before beside Frankie's father, who had passed away the previous November. The choir sang "Amazing Grace," "Wind Beneath My Wings" and "Go Rest High On That Mountain."

At the end, the minister even mentioned Morris the cat. "So far, Morris seems to be keeping a low profile," the minister said. "But please keep an eye out for him. And if you catch sight of him, please call Jace Abernathy." And she read off his phone number. "Jace has provided flyers on that table near the door. Be sure to grab one on your way out."

When Tamara got up to go, she spotted her friend Stephanie on the arm of her rodeo-star fiancé, Geoff Burris. Stephanie waved her over. They went down the church steps together and stopped to talk a little at the bottom. All around them, other people spoke softly in small groups, many of them clutching flyers about Melissa's missing cat.

As for Tamara and her friends, they said the stuff you say at times like this—how lovely the service had been and what a beautiful day for it.

Like Tamara, Stephanie was blinking back tears. Geoff put his arm around her, and she leaned into his tall, solid strength.

Watching them together, so happy, with a life of love and family ahead of them, Tamara couldn't help but feel a little bit…well, not envious, exactly. But sad with a faint hint of yearning that things hadn't worked out as well for her.

Maybe someday...

Or maybe not.

Drawing her shoulders back, she reminded herself that she had work she loved, a home of her own and good friends like Stephanie. Her life was full and she had no complaints. There was even Harley, who purred every time he caught sight of her. He was right there, cuddling close, whenever she needed him to listen to her doubts and her fears.

"Tamara. Hey!"

Jace's deep, warm voice made the butterflies take flight in her belly—which was ludicrous.

How could there be butterflies? There was absolutely nothing going on between her and Jace. He wanted her help in his effort to foster Frankie, and somehow he'd managed to get her on board with that.

It was not a butterflies-in-the-belly situation.

But still, she could feel them, fluttering around in there, all atwitter at the mere sound of that man's voice.

When she turned to him, she realized she was wearing a great big smile. "Jace. Hey."

"I was hoping to catch you." He was?

She introduced him to Stephanie and he tipped his white hat. "Nice to meet you," he said in that easy way of his. Then he turned to her fiancé. "Geoff," he said as the two men shook hands. "Good to see you again. It's been a while." Of course Jace knew Geoff, she thought. Geoff was a big rodeo star, and he probably knew all the Abernathys.

Geoff said, "We need to get together for a beer one of these days."

"Anytime," said Jace. "Let me know."

For a few minutes the four of them remained at the base of the church steps chatting about nothing in particular.

Then Stephanie said she and Geoff had to get going. Stepping in close, she gave Tamara a quick hug and whispered for her ears alone, "Have fun."

"Stop," she whispered back.

Stephanie put on her sweetest smile for Jace. "Bye, Jace." She waved as she and Geoff walked off toward the parking lot.

Jace said, "Barbecue tonight out at my folks' house on the Bonnie B. I really want you to be there." She opened her mouth to say she couldn't, but he put up a hand. "I know, you said you have errands. So I'll pick you up at six."

"Jace, I—"

He leaned close. "Just say yes."

"Yes." The pesky word escaped her lips before she could call it back.

"Terrific—and now I'm going to get out of here before you have a chance to change your mind. See you at six."

"Harley, tell me to get myself under control."

Her cat, perched at the foot of her bed with half the clothes from her closet in a messy pile behind him, purred louder than ever and regarded her through lazy-lidded eyes.

In a white lace bra and panties to match, Tamara braced her fists on her hips and glared. "He'll be here any minute. I desperately need to decide what to wear."

Still purring, Harley lifted one sleek black paw and began to give that paw a bath. With a groan of frustration, Tamara stepped to the side of the bed and rifled through the pile of clothing. She ended up grabbing a snug pair of bootcut jeans and a feather-light pink Western shirt with white piping. Next, she returned to her closet for her favorite orchid ankle boots with an etched metal toe.

She held them up for Harley's approval. "Too fancy?" Harley flopped onto his side and yawned. "Okay then. You love them and think they're just right." Harley set to work washing his other front paw. "Excellent. We are in complete agreement, then."

Five minutes later when she answered the door, Jace swept off his hat and gave her a long, slow look from the top of her head to the metal tips on the toes of her purple boots. "Tamara Hanson," he said almost reverently, "you look beautiful."

"Thank you—and this is not a date," she reminded him, feeling instantly foolish for making a big deal of it.

He shook his head. "Nope. Not a date." His fine mouth curved in a great big smile. "But you can't blame a man for admiring the view."

He offered his arm and off they went.

At the Bonnie B, the family barbecue took up most of the big open field beyond the landscaped area in front of the large main house. There were three smokers and a couple of grills filling the air with the scent of slow-smoked ribs and juicy steak. Beneath tall cottonwoods near a rustic wooden fence, long picnic tables covered with bright checked table-cloths invited everyone to grab a plate, take a seat and dig in.

Abernathys were everywhere. Jace introduced her to cousins and aunts and uncles. She met Jace's brothers and sisters, his two nephews and his niece, and also his mom and his dad, Asa.

Asa Abernathy was tall and broad shouldered like his sons. Tamara found herself thinking that Jace had inherited his dad's warm, sincere smile.

As for Jace's mom, Bonnie Abernathy was nothing short of a force of nature.

When Jace introduced them, he said, "Mom, this is Tamara. She's the nurse who took care of Frankie at Bronco Valley Hospital the day he was born. She's also the one who shopped long and hard with me yesterday, making sure I have everything I need to take good care of Frankie when he moves in."

Bonnie caught Tamara's hand and cradled it between both of hers. "It's a pleasure, Tamara. You call me Bonnie, you hear?"

"Good to meet you, too, Bonnie."

"A nurse," Bonnie said approvingly. "Tamara, it's so wonderful of you to help Jace with this. He's very determined once he sets his mind to something, but surrounding himself with skilled, knowledgeable people who can vouch with authority for his fitness as a father? It matters, Tamara. It matters a lot."

Tamara shot Jace a quick glance. He was grinning. And then she heard herself confessing, "I have to admit, I wasn't so sure Jace should get custody. Not at first."

"You weren't?" Was Bonnie offended for her son—or intrigued? Tamara couldn't decide.

Jace spoke up then. "Yeah, Mom. Tamara had all kinds of doubts about me."

"I see." Bonnie let Tamara's hand go.

"In my defense," Tamara offered, "my doubts weren't really about Jace in particular."

Bonnie was definitely frowning now. "Then who *were* your doubts about?"

Tamara met the older woman's sharp eyes directly. "It's just that I'm sure there are a lot of couples— good people who've waited too long already for a child, people who are fully prepared right now to give Frankie a loving two-parent home. It seems a little unfair that Jace is going to be able to…cut in line ahead of them, I guess you could say."

Bonnie looked thoughtful. And then she nodded. "You're right, of course. A healthy newborn would have no problem finding a loving home. Frankie would probably be adopted right away by one of the couples you're talking about—but the dying wish of Frankie's mother has to be considered too. In fact,

Melissa Smith's wishes for her child matter a great deal."

"You're right, Bonnie. And I have been thinking about that, about what Melissa wanted for her baby. It counts for a lot."

"Good, then. I'm glad we understand each other. I'm also grateful you're on board to help my son with this. And I honestly look forward to getting to know you better, Tamara." With a final, bright smile, Bonnie set off through the low grass toward the tables under the trees.

Tamara watched her go. "Wow. Your mom is…"

"Intense? Opinionated? Absolutely certain that she knows best?" Jace let out a low rumble of good-natured laughter. "Right on all counts. The good news is, if she likes you, she'll do anything for you." He lowered his voice for her ears alone. "And she likes you, Tamara. She likes you a lot." He grabbed her hand. "Now, come on. I want you to meet Stacy."

The barbecue lasted until after midnight. Tamara had a great time. By the end, she sat at a table talking to Robin about her work with horses, as she idly petted Jace's two big, sweet dogs who had decided to flop down at her feet.

Jace got her home at a little before one.

He walked her to her door.

They stood on the welcome mat, facing each other. The porch light brought out streaks of auburn in his thick brown hair. She imagined reaching up, running her fingers through the gleaming strands, feeling the silky texture against her skin—and boy, was she letting her thoughts roam way out of line, or what? They'd agreed they were friend-zoned. She would not be running her fingers through Jace's hair.

He asked, "Do you have to work tomorrow?"

"Yep. Seven to seven."

"A.m. to p.m.?"

"That's right."

"I have to work, too. Tomorrow's my weekly shift at the firehouse. It's also seven to seven, but round-the-clock. I won't get home till Monday morning."

She gazed up into his eyes and thought about kissing him—yet another more-than-friends activity she shouldn't be imagining. And the look in his eyes made her wonder if he might be thinking about kissing her, too.

The warm summer night seemed to shimmer around them. "Friends," she whispered, trying to sound firm and not really succeeding.

"Yeah." He took off his hat. "I remember."

"Thank you for tonight, Jace. I had a wonderful time, and it was so good to meet your family."

"Tonight's been great. I hate to see it end." Then, as if he remembered something, he asked, "Do you always work twelve-hour shifts?"

"Not always. My schedule changes because I'm okay with filling in where I'm needed. Tomorrow I'm on duty till seven, but the rest of this coming week, I clock out at three."

He put on a sad look. "You're going to miss the Miss Bronco Beauty Pageant tomorrow." The beauty contest kicked off Bronco's annual Fourth of July celebration, Red, White and Bronco.

She shrugged. "You'll miss it, too."

"Can't be helped—and I'll call you Monday afternoon." His slow smile made promises she had to be careful not to let him keep. He must have read the wariness in her eyes because he put on an innocent tone and added, "I mean, I do need your help. There's so much to do."

Yes, there was.

And she wasn't sure how long she could go on telling herself that this was only about a sweet, orphaned baby.

Not that she would back out. Even though her attraction to him had started to feel kind of dangerous, she was in this now. She'd agreed to help him, and she would keep her word. "Whatever you need, Jace. Let me know."

"Oh, I will."

Say good night, her wiser self advised. *Say good night and go inside.*

But she just stood there in the warm glow of her porch light, smiling up at him as he stared down at her.

It was lovely, really, this feeling that she wasn't

supposed to be having, this feeling that they were somehow falling into each other, slowly, weightlessly. An endless, floating, mutual descent to a thrilling and tender collision.

Her breath was coming faster. She felt heat in her cheeks. Her body swayed closer to him...

Uh-uh. She straightened her spine. *Not going to happen.*

Pulling her house key from her pocket, she held it up like it could serve as a barrier between them. "'Night, Jace," she said firmly.

He drew a slow breath and let it out carefully. "Night."

Hands in his pockets, he ran down the steps, turning on his heel at the bottom to walk backward to his waiting crew cab, holding her gaze all the way.

Jace's Sunday to Monday shift at the firehouse went by in a flash. He cooked and cleaned. They went on three calls—a medical emergency in Bronco Heights, another in Bronco Valley and a brush fire on a ten-acre ranchette a couple of miles from town.

All three calls ended well—meaning there were no structures burned in the brush fire and there was no loss of life. The elderly man who'd collapsed in his Bronco Heights home was spending a couple of days in the hospital and expected to fully recover. The ten-year-old girl in Bronco Valley who fell out of the oak tree in her backyard had a closed nondisplaced fracture of her left humerus. She would be wearing a splint for a while and good as new in eight weeks.

Starting at seven Monday morning when Jace's shift at the station ended, it was all about Frankie. He met with his caseworker at nine, went to a meeting with his group of prospective foster parents at eleven, and then spent a couple of hours in the early afternoon studying the reams of material he'd been assigned to get him up to speed on becoming a foster dad.

He called Tamara at a little past three. "I sure could use some help whipping Frankie's room into shape."

She didn't hesitate and that pleased him to no end. "I'll get changed, feed my cat and be right over."

"I'll come get you."

"Nope. I have my own car, I know how to drive it and I know where you live."

"But I don't mind—"

"Jace. I'll be there by four."

And she was. Bailey and Luna loped out to greet her. She spent a few minutes petting them and telling them how wonderful they were.

Inside, he gave her a quick tour of the place. "Two nice big bedrooms downstairs and two more upstairs. It's a large cabin, Jace."

"You don't like it?"

"It's beautiful. I just pictured something smaller—

but I think it's terrific that you have a room for Frankie right next to the master suite."

"Exactly." Frankie's room had previously been the guest room he rarely used. He'd already moved all that furniture upstairs. "It's going to work out just great."

With the dogs sprawled nearby, they put Frankie's crib together, hung shelves and moved the new baby furniture around. They put away blankets and onesies, stacked diapers on the shelves mounted over the new changing table and made a decal mural on one wall—a farm scene with smiling cows, dancing sheep and happy horses. There were fat clouds in the sky and a rainbow that arched over Frankie's crib.

"Hungry?" Jace asked his favorite nurse at a little after seven.

"I should probably—"

"Uh-uh." He cut her off before she could start talking about leaving. "Don't even think about it. I put a chicken in the slow cooker when I got home this morning. You need to share it with me before you even think about heading back into town."

Tamara stayed for the chicken. After the meal, she said yes to a decaf. He kept her talking until nine and then walked her out to her little SUV.

She got in and he shut the door. When she rolled down the window, he said, "Thank you."

She gave him that glowing smile. "It was fun."

He leaned in a little closer and considered making

his move, going in for a goodbye kiss. But he held back. They were friends, he reminded himself. She didn't want more.

Yet.

"See you tomorrow," she said. "I'll be here at four, same as today."

He stood waving as she drove away, thinking that tomorrow couldn't come fast enough.

As promised, she showed up right on time Tuesday. By seven, they'd added a second mural on the wall opposite the one behind the crib and filled another bureau with baby stuff. Frankie's room was officially whipped into shape.

"Let's go into town," he said. "After all, it's the Fourth of July. There's the big barbecue in Bronco Park. There will be fireworks and dancing later."

"You know I have to work tomorrow," she reminded him.

"I know you do, but I have a plan."

"What plan?"

"I'll follow you in. We'll get some ribs and watch the fireworks. And then just a dance or two afterward. You'll be home by eleven."

Still, she hesitated. "I shouldn't..."

He kept after her and refused to feel guilty about it. "Eleven, I promise you."

Finally, she agreed to his plan.

Jace smiled all the way into town. When she pulled into her driveway, she signaled for him to park his truck beside her little SUV. Together, they walked the few blocks to the park. He almost reached for her hand as they strolled along. But once again, he reminded himself that getting too cozy right now wouldn't work in his favor.

At Bronco Park, they joined Stephanie Brandt and Geoff Burris at a table not far from the outdoor stage where Miss Bronco had been crowned two nights before. Geoff's brother Mike, a med student who used to ride the rodeos with the rest of the Burris family, sat with them, along with another Burris brother, Jack, and his fiancée, Audrey Hawkins. Like Geoff, Jack was a rodeo star. Audrey, too. Her family was every bit as legendary on the rodeo circuit as the Burris brothers. Back in the day, Audrey's mom and her aunts had billed themselves as the Hawkins Sisters and taken medals and purses in rodeos all over the western states.

Stephanie and Tamara joked that they could almost feel intimidated, hanging around with all the big rodeo stars.

Mike Burris, the med student, argued that their table was half medical personnel and the rodeo people had to respect that—especially when one of them got injured on the job.

"I'll raise my root beer to that," said Stephanie.

Everybody joined in the toast.

It was a great night. They all watched the fireworks together.

And finally, Jace got to hold Tamara in his arms for a slow dance under the stars. He got extra lucky when the band played two slow ones back-to-back. He just kept on holding her and swaying to the music and she didn't object.

The town psychic, Winona Cobbs, still slim and spry in her nineties, danced near them in the arms of her fiancé, Stanley Sanchez. Folks in town joked that Winona had landed herself a "younger" man. After all, Stanley was only in his eighties.

"Such a lovely couple," Winona said as she and Stanley danced a little closer to where Jace held Tamara in his arms.

He glanced over to meet Winona's wise eyes.

"Yes, I do mean you," the psychic said—so softly that no one else seemed to hear. Then she and Stanley danced away.

Jace gathered Tamara a little bit closer. She felt so good in his arms, a small package and a beautiful one.

He thought about Winona's words.

Were he and Tamara a couple?

How could they be? They'd yet to even share a kiss. Plus, she'd friend-zoned him out of the gate.

But the truth was, Jace already felt like they were together, a team.

Yeah, they were "just friends." But that didn't stop him from he wanting to spend every moment he could with her.

She glanced up at him with a dreamy smile.

Damn. He wanted to kiss her.

"You have the strangest look on your face," she said. "What are you thinking?"

He bent close. "It's a secret."

She laughed. "Tell me."

"Can't."

She scoffed. "You mean you won't."

He only smiled.

And she let it go.

On the walk back to her house, it took a lot of effort not to reach for her hand. But he held himself back. He took her up to her door and said a friendly, "Good night."

And then he drove home, wondering how long he could last before he threw caution to the wind and made a damn move.

Chapter Five

At home, Jace kept thinking of Tamara. He didn't get to sleep till after one.

Two hours later, his pager went off. He threw on his clothes and headed for a barn fire ten miles from the Bonnie B. The barn burned to the ground, but they at least managed to get all the animals out. He followed the crew to the station to help with cleanup.

Back at his cabin at ten in the morning, he fell across his bed and went out like a light. After three hours of sleep, he had work to do. He got out the material he needed to know by heart in order to be prepared to make a good home for Frankie and he studied till six.

Tamara showed up at six-thirty.

He offered dinner. As they ate, they went over his checklist for the home study visit the next day.

His mother dropped by. She claimed she just wanted to make sure he was ready for tomorrow, but her real objective was crystal clear to him. She'd come over to get another look at Tamara.

And judging by her too-wide smile and eager nods at everything Tamara said, Bonnie Abernathy had already reached the conclusion that Tamara Hanson was exactly the kind of woman she hoped Jace might get together with—a woman with a generous heart and meaningful work of her own.

Bonnie's approval was painfully obvious, which embarrassed him a little. But really, he had nothing to complain about. He wanted Tamara, and his mom heartily approved of her.

Before Bonnie left, she caught his eye. He knew exactly what she was thinking—that Tamara was a keeper and he needed to make sure she didn't get away.

Jace kissed his mom's cheek and ushered her out the door. She meant well, but sometimes she could be downright overbearing.

Well, she could push all she wanted. He refused to let her pressure him about this. He would make a move when the time was right—or more likely, when he couldn't stand not to.

For now, he got to hang out with his favorite nurse every day. They really were becoming friends, and friendship was a big step in the right direction. He told himself not to jump the gun, that everything would work out as it should.

That night alone in his bed, he had trouble sleeping. Tomorrow was the home study. It needed to go well.

He thought about Melissa, tried to picture her happy in heaven with Frankie's dad, Kenny.

And then he started feeling guilty about Morris the cat. A full week had passed since he put up the flyers around Melissa's neighborhood. And then there were the flyers he'd left at the memorial service on Saturday. No one had gotten back to him with information about the missing cat. It almost seemed as though Morris had vanished off the face of the earth.

He reminded himself yet again that the home study visit was tomorrow. He needed to keep his focus on that.

But at eight the next morning, he drove into town to Melissa's building. He went up and down the stairs, knocking on doors, asking anyone who answered if they'd seen any sign of the cat. He talked to the construction guys at work in the damaged units.

But nobody had spotted Melissa's missing tabby.

It was discouraging, but Jace didn't know what else to do about Morris right now.

He returned to the ranch at a little after ten for the home study visit, which was scheduled for eleven. Tamara's car was parked in front of his cabin. Looking like a million bucks in dark-washed jeans and a pretty silk shirt, she waved at him from the front porch, where she sat in one of the Adirondack chairs with Luna on one side and Bailey on the other.

"I thought you had to work," he said as he ran up the steps. The dogs met him and he crouched to greet them.

"I got the day off." She gave him a big, happy smile.

His heart seemed to expand in his chest, causing the sweetest sort of ache. It meant a lot that she'd found a way to be here when he needed her most.

He wanted to yank her out of that chair, wrap her up in his hungry arms and kiss the ever-loving daylights right out of her.

Not yet, he reminded himself for the umpteenth time. "I'm really glad you're here for this." He said the words quietly, with feeling. "In case I haven't made it clear enough—thank you for all your help."

"You're welcome." She gave him that beautiful smile. "How're you feeling?"

"Nervous."

"Don't be. You're ready. It's going to go great."

Five minutes later, his mom arrived. They were a one-two punch, Tamara and his mom. Having them beside him would strike just the right note for the woman from Child and Family Services. She would see that he had capable, knowledgeable people around him to help him navigate instant fatherhood.

The social worker drove up right on time. Jace gave her a tour of the cabin. The woman played it cool. He had no idea what she was thinking as he showed her his place and the room that was all fixed up, ready for Frankie.

Bailey and Luna were on their very best behavior—but then they were always that way, calm and affectionate. They aimed to please. When the caseworker paused to pet them and ask for their names, they both sat at attention and gazed up at her adoringly.

The caseworker already knew his mother.

When he introduced her to Tamara, she asked, "Do you live here on the ranch, then?"

"No," said Tamara. "I'm a nurse. Jace asked me to help him out with the home study."

The social worker slid a puzzled glance at Jace. "You're aware that this visit is just for family and caregivers?"

He was ready for that one. "I am, yes. And Tamara specializes in maternal/child nursing at Bronco Valley Hospital. She was on duty the day Frankie was born. She cared for him when the ambulance brought him and his mother in.

"And I have to tell you, she was kind and patient with me when I came storming into reception, covered in soot from the fire, demanding to know where the mother and the baby were. She settled me down and then let me see Frankie—and then later, she agreed to help me get ready for today."

His explanation seemed to satisfy the social worker. She smiled and shook Tamara's hand.

They all sat in the living room for a while. The woman asked questions and Jace answered. He'd done his homework and none of the questions threw him. He thought he was coming off as confident and well prepared—at least, he hoped so. Because the entire time, he was a wreck inside, sure he would somehow mess up.

His sisters and brothers, who'd all turned in information to Child and Family Services as family members willing to help out with Frankie, came over one by one to meet the social worker. She interviewed each of them briefly.

The whole thing took six endless hours.

As the woman was leaving, she promised that he would know within the next week whether or not he would be allowed to foster Frankie.

He wanted to beg her to please make it happen faster, to argue that Frankie needed a permanent home as soon as possible. But he had to get real about this. Frankie's home here on the Bonnie B wouldn't be considered permanent, anyway—not until Jace legally adopted him. Plus, it was just not a good idea to nag the social worker.

But damn. He could barely keep his mouth shut about it. Every time he got the urge to start in on her, he reminded himself that he was already on the fastest of fast tracks. Pushing harder wouldn't help and would probably work against him.

When she was finally gone, his mother grabbed him in a hug. "You did well, son."

"I hope so. She seemed...really cool about the whole visit."

"That's her job," his mom reassured him. "You've got nothing to worry about."

Tamara was nodding. "And you'll know next week." He must have sent her a panicked glance because she put up both hands and added in a soothing voice, "Not that there's any question about it. I'm sure it will go in your favor."

"You've done the work," his mom declared. She stepped away as Tamara moved closer. "Ahem..." Now his mom had a secret little smile on her face. "I really need to get back to the house."

Jace almost laughed. Could she be any more obvious? His mom heartily approved of everything about his favorite nurse, and that had her falling all over herself to leave them alone together.

Which was A-OK with him. "Thanks again, Mom."

His mother couldn't resist gushing just a little bit more. "Tamara, it was so good of you to be here today."

"I wanted to be here, Bonnie. I really did."

"And we do appreciate that. We can't tell you how much."

Okay, this was getting weird. "Bye, Mom."

"Ahem. Yes, right. I'll see you two later." And off she went down the steps.

When she was out of earshot, Tamara stepped closer and asked, "Is your mom okay?"

"Absolutely. She's just really excited about all this."

"Ah. Well, I can understand that."

"And don't I get a hug from you?"

"Of course." She moved in even closer. He wrapped her in his arms, felt her softness against him, breathed in that clean, sweet scent that belonged only to her and thought about the beautiful possibility of never letting go.

Too soon, she was pulling away. "Listen, I really should get home and—"

"Stay. Please. I'll grill us some steaks."

"I shouldn't."

"Yes, you should. And I won't take no for an answer."

Tamara knew that she really ought to head back to town. She'd switched her days off, and that meant she would be on shift at seven tomorrow morning.

But come on. Jace wanted her to stay and she wanted to celebrate with him. The home study visit had gone so well. She had very little doubt now that Jace would accomplish the impossible and become Frankie's dad.

"Stay," he said again. "Please."

Her resistance melted. "Only if you let me help."

"I would love help. Cut up the salad?"

"Of course."

Jace grilled the steaks out behind the cabin, but clouds had gathered as the evening approached. By the time the food was ready, the wind was up and a light rain made everything misty.

They ate at the big, roughhewn kitchen table inside. The steaks were delicious, and he opened a nice bottle of red wine.

"To you and Frankie," she offered as a toast. He clinked his glass with hers.

After the meal, she accepted more wine and they sat on the big sofa by the stone fireplace.

He said, "Tell me about you, Tamara."

"You'll need to narrow the subject down a little. What, exactly, do you want to know about me?"

He gazed at her so steadily, his eyes mossy green now, as soft as some secret, sheltered place in the middle of a forest. "So, then. Last Friday night at Doug's, you said you've never been married."

"That's right. I haven't."

"Any serious relationships?"

"Four." Before he could coax her to elaborate, she turned the tables on him. "You?"

He looked into his glass and then had a small sip. "More than four."

She wasn't letting him off the hook. "How many?"

"Six—and yeah. It's a lot. I know that. For a long

time, I was caught in a loop, you might say, wanting to help *too* much. I chose women with problems, women I thought needed saving, and the relationships never got past a certain point."

"What point?"

"The point where I wanted more—but I had chosen someone who had trouble taking care of herself. The complaints would start. That I wasn't there for her, that I needed to give up football, firefighting, everything else in my life, and just concentrate on her. So we would break up, and a year or two later, I would meet someone new, someone having a hard time, someone who was looking for a helping hand and…"

"The cycle would start all over again?"

"Yeah." He met her gaze, his eyes steady.

She didn't know what to think. "Are you trying to tell me that you somehow see me as having a hard time, as needing a helping hand?"

"What?" He sat back against the leather sofa cushion, frowning. "No way. I see you as strong and self-reliant, the kind of woman who runs her own life and does a damn fine job of it. Also, hot. I see you as a real smoke show."

She laughed then—partly in relief that he didn't see her as needy. And, yeah, maybe a little bit because she loved that he'd called her hot. Even if that was borderline inappropriate, given that she kept trying to tell both him and herself that they were friends and nothing more.

"So how about those four guys?" he suggested hopefully.

"Well, I had a boyfriend in high school. We split up after graduation. I would say that was mutual. We grew out of each other. Then there was someone in college. That was more…problematic."

"Okay, that doesn't sound good."

She admitted, "Because it's not, really."

"Now I hate that guy." He pulled his knee up on the cushion and rested his arm along the sofa back. "What happened?"

"He borrowed a thousand dollars from me, broke up with me to get back together with his high school sweetheart—and never did pay me the money he owed me."

"What a loser."

"Yeah. I decided to call it a win, though. I mean, he cost me a thousand bucks, but at least he was out of my life, right?"

"That's the spirit." He leaned a fraction closer. She got a whiff of his outdoorsy scent—like leather and wood shavings. Everything about him appealed to her. That made him dangerous.

And yet, there she sat, holding his gaze, slowly sipping her second glass of wine.

He asked, "Relationship number three?"

"He was a fellow nurse. A nurse with a drug problem, as it turned out—and he was stealing his supply from the Southern California hospital where we both worked. Took me months to put it together. When I did, I turned him in."

"Good for you."

"After him, I decided I needed a change. That's when I took the job here in Bronco."

"And I am so damn glad you did." He was clearly waiting for her to tell him about the fourth guy.

No way was she giving him any specifics about Eric. "Number four cheated."

Jace tipped his head to the side, studying her. "What a bastard."

"Exactly."

"You're well rid of him."

"Yes, I am." She shifted to set her glass on the coffee table—and also to get a little distance from the compelling man beside her. "Essentially, my trust in men is dust right now."

"Hey…"

She sat back with a sigh and stared him straight in the eye. "What?"

"I guess it's good you didn't mention any names."

"Why is that?"

"Well, the guy in high school gets a pass from me. It sounds like you were both on the same page about calling it quits."

"We were."

"But the other three? I have a bad urge to pay each one a visit."

"Not your job, Jace."

He drew in a slow breath and nodded. "You're right—but that doesn't stop me from wanting to do a little damage to any man who's hurt you." He surprised her with a slow smile. "There is good news here, though."

"And what's that?"

"If you were still with one of them, how would I ever get a chance with you?"

There was a moment when they just stared at each other.

And then she shook herself. "Jace, I'm really not willing to get involved with anyone right now."

He looked at her intently. "I know."

The big room was so quiet suddenly.

The silence thickened. They both leaned in at the same time.

I am not going to kiss you, she thought as his warm, soft mouth met hers.

"I know," he whispered against her parted lips, and she wondered if she'd said she wouldn't kiss him out loud. But then he added, "It's too soon for kisses. I get it." And she decided that she hadn't said the words out loud. Instead, he was mentally on the same page with her.

And she liked the idea of that so much—that they

might be attuned somehow, able to sense what the other was thinking.

She made a sound, something midway between a sigh and a happy little moan.

Really, she could not believe this. Hadn't she just flat-out said she would not get romantically involved with him?

His mouth moved on hers, brushing gently.

It felt so good. So right.

His tongue teased at her parted lips.

Blame it on the wine, on the open, honest way he looked at her, on the tenderness in his leaf-green eyes. On the way he listened when she spoke, the way he really did seem to be a whole different kind of man than she'd been with up till now—not that she was *with* him.

She wasn't. She was...

Her thoughts scattered as he deepened the kiss. His big arms went around her and she melted right into his broad, hard chest.

Wonderful. Delicious.

Jace Abernathy took kissing to a whole new level.

Oh, she could get used to this. She could stay here with him on this sofa all night, just kissing and kissing, melting right into him as he rubbed her back with those big hands and cradled her like she was infinitely precious—something so special and rare.

She hadn't even realized she'd closed her eyes

until he brushed his lips against hers and gently lifted that wonderful mouth away.

Then she was blinking up at him, dazed. "I really wasn't going to kiss you," she said.

"I know." He grinned then. "Sorry."

"No you're not." She frowned. "What?"

He tipped his head toward the center of the room. She followed his gaze.

Luna and Bailey sat on the far side of the coffee table, side by side, watching them intently.

That broke the spell he'd somehow woven around her.

They both started laughing. The dogs got up and came around on either side of the coffee table. Jace cuddled Luna and Tamara lavished attention on Bailey.

When she looked up from smooching Bailey, he was watching her.

"Gotta go," she said.

He walked her out to her car.

She promised herself she wasn't going to kiss him if he reached for her again.

But he didn't. He opened her door for her. She got in and he said, "Buckle up."

She drove away reminding herself that she wasn't the least disappointed he'd made no effort to kiss her goodbye.

At home, she put on a sleep shirt and shorts,

grabbed the terrific mystery novel she'd started last night and climbed into bed to read herself to sleep.

But her focus was shot. When Harley jumped up to join her on the bed, she put the book aside. Harley snuggled up close, and she leaned back against the pillows, stroking the cat, trying really hard not to think about that kiss.

"I'm not falling for him," she said to Harley, who never argued, only purred louder when she shared her secrets with him. "Absolutely not. We're just friends. That's all it is, all it's ever going to be. It was just one of those things. A kiss. Nothing. Meaningless—and never going to happen again."

Harley tipped his head back. She wasn't sure she liked that knowing look in his tawny eyes—like he didn't believe a single word she said.

She was about to insist that she meant it, she really did. That nothing had happened and nothing *would* happen.

But the more she argued that it was nothing, the more she felt foolish about the whole thing.

She gave Harley a kiss between the ears, turned off the light and closed her eyes.

Sometime later, the ringing of her phone woke her.

With a groan, she sat up and grabbed it off the nightstand.

"Great," she muttered, as she blinked at the display. "Mom."

She considered letting it go to voice mail, but her

mom had a habit of calling late on a weeknight. If Tamara called her back the next day, she wouldn't answer. She would simply call again tomorrow night or the night after, most likely when Tamara was in bed asleep. In her mom's defense, it was an hour earlier in California. And Olivia was probably feeling a little lonely. Tamara's current stepdad was always off somewhere wheeling and dealing.

Tamara took the call. "Hi, Mom."

"There you are. You sound tired."

"I was asleep."

"Are you all right?"

"Of course."

"Tamara Lynn, you don't sound all right. And I've been thinking—"

"Mom, I really am fine. Just half-asleep, that's all. How are you?"

"No complaints. Nigel is off in Las Vegas for a few days. It's quiet here, but I don't mind. I had a lovely, relaxing day at the spa." Her mom spent a lot of time at the spa and enjoying long lunches with her friends, lunches that usually included a few glasses of white wine. "And I called because I started thinking how, now that the thing with the doctor is over, there really is no reason for you to remain way up there in the wilds of Montana."

"I love it here."

"You're just being stubborn."

"No, I'm being honest. And come on, Bronco is

not the 'wilds.' We have indoor plumbing and electricity, grocery stores and Wi-Fi."

"Sarcasm is unnecessary. You know what I mean."

"Mom, I'm not moving to Palm Springs."

"But a change would do you good. I want you to be happy."

"I *am* happy."

"Oh, darling. You're smart and caring and pretty. You could so easily have it all. Nigel and I know many wealthy, powerful men who are looking for the right kind of wife."

"How many ways can I say this to you? What you're looking for in life is not what I'm looking for."

"Oh, darling. Everyone wants comfort and security. I know, I know. You're only thirty-one, but you really shouldn't waste any time if you know what I mean. The years go by so fast. If you will only let me introduce you to the kind of man who will know how to take care of you, you can give up those twelve-hour shifts at the hospital helping other women give birth to their babies and have some beautiful babies of your own."

Tamara reminded herself that, as conversations with her mother went, this one was nothing out of the ordinary. "I love it here, Mom. I mean that. And I would appreciate it if you would take my word for it."

"But—"

"I am exactly where I want to be, and I have no interest in finding a man right now." It bugged her to no end that she thought of Jace at that moment—Jace and his kindness, his determination to do the right thing. Jace with his big arms and corrugated abs and that bone-melting kiss they'd shared earlier.

"I just want you to think about coming home, darling."

"I am home, Mom."

"You are so obstinate. Come for a visit, won't you? Soon? I miss you."

"I miss you, too." She knew her mom was lonely. Olivia had a lot of casual friends but no one she could really talk to. And Nigel was always somewhere else. He did seem to adore her mother, but he was gone way too much. Sometimes Tamara wondered how long marriage number four would last. "I can't come to see you for a while, though." She'd flown out for six days the first week of June. "Maybe at Christmas."

"Darling, Christmas is months away."

"You could come here, Mom. The guest room is ready and waiting for you."

"I don't think so."

"Well, if you change your mind, you are always welcome."

Twenty minutes later, her mom finally said goodbye. Tamara put the phone down and turned off the bedside lamp. Yeah, conversations with her mother often went badly. But tonight, Tamara felt she'd held her own against Olivia's relentless efforts to get her to move to Palm Springs and snag herself a rich husband.

She worried for her mom. Olivia just wasn't happy. Tamara, on the other hand, was feeling pretty good about her life tonight.

Yeah, the thing with Eric had been awful. But that was behind her now. As each day went by, it became more and more obvious that she'd dodged a bullet with him, pure and simple.

As for Jace Abernathy...

Well, okay, she probably shouldn't have kissed him. But she really did enjoy his company, and she felt good now to be helping him keep his promise to Melissa Smith.

She'd truly meant what she'd said to her mom on the phone. She loved living in Bronco. No way would she consider living anywhere else. To the sound of Harley's contented purring, she drifted back to sleep.

The next day at the hospital, she and Stephanie had lunch together. They got sandwiches in the cafeteria and went outside to sit in the tree-shaded courtyard to eat.

"So," said her friend. "You and Jace Abernathy...?"

Tamara enjoyed a bite of her turkey on rye. Though she'd seen her friend Saturday after the memorial service and then again on the Fourth, they really hadn't had much chance to talk. "It's a friend thing with Jace," she said.

Stephanie mic-dropped her half sandwich without taking a bite. "You think I buy that? Tamara, this is me you're talking to."

"Honestly, I've been helping him to get certified to foster Frankie, that's all." Her conscience called her a liar. So what? One kiss did not a budding romance make.

"Please." Stephanie sat back and folded her arms across her middle. "That was helping him to get custody, the two of you slow dancing at the barbecue Tuesday night?"

"What? Friends aren't allowed to slow dance?"

"Sure, they are. But when friends slow dance together they look nothing like you and Jace looked Tuesday night."

She should let that go—but then she didn't. "And what did Jace and I look like, exactly?"

"Closer than you had to be. Intimate. Cuddly. Show me two *friends* who look cuddly when they slow dance."

"We were not cuddly."

"Oh, yeah. You were."

"You are so far off base about this."

"If I'm off base, it's because I've left third behind and I'm sprinting for home—but okay. Let's say I'm wrong and you are just friends with Jace Abernathy." Stephanie picked up her half sandwich again and took a bite.

"I really am helping him—to get custody of Frankie, I mean."

Stephanie chewed and swallowed before muttering, "I believe you, absolutely."

"Great. Can we move on?"

"Good idea."

"Yesterday was the home study visit."

Stephanie nodded and put on a bright smile. "How'd it go?"

"Really well. His mom was there. Each of his brothers and sisters came by individually to talk to the caseworker, too. Jace was ready, fully prepared. He had all the right answers to the caseworker's questions, and he meant every one of them. I've just…never met anyone like him before. He's so…"

Stephanie had set down her sandwich again. Her expression was serious and interested. But there was also a definite gleam in her eye.

"Don't say it," Tamara commanded softly.

"I wouldn't dare. I did talk to Geoff about him, though. Geoff knows the Abernathys pretty well."

Now Tamara was the one leaning in. "What did he say?"

"He said the oldest brother, Billy, did some serious bronc riding back in the day, so Geoff knew him from the circuit and got to know his family a little, too. Geoff says that Asa and Bonnie's sons are all good guys…"

"But?"

"Billy's long divorced and Theo's definitely living the bachelor life. As for Jace, well, Geoff says he's been in several relationships, but none of them have lasted."

Tamara thought about the things Jace had said last night. "We, uh, talked about that, Jace and me."

"About all his past girlfriends?"

"In a general way, yeah." She didn't want to betray Jace's confidence, not even to Stephanie.

Her friend seemed to pick up her reluctance to share any details. "Well, whatever he said, you seem good with it."

"I believe what he told me. And, hey, my relationships haven't lasted, either."

Stephanie grinned. "I knew it. You like him. Admit it."

Tamara pressed her lips together. A change of subject wouldn't hurt about now. "As I said, Jace and I are friends—and it was fun the other night. That's the first time I've met Geoff's brother Mike."

"So I take it we are through discussing you and the sexy ranching firefighter?" Stephanie asked in a teasing tone.

"Yes, we are. Tell me about Mike."

"Sure. Mike's doing well in medical school, but Geoff says Mike has some problems in his love life."

"What kind of problems?"

"Now I'm the one who doesn't want to betray a confidence. I'll just say Geoff seems convinced that

Mike will work it out—and for the record, I like Jace. I think you ought to give the guy a chance."

Jace called at eight that evening as Tamara sat on the sofa, remote in hand, scanning her Netflix options.

Her silly heart was racing when she answered. "Hi!" She dropped the remote onto the coffee table and stood up. "Any news?"

He chuckled, a deep, sexy sound, and reminded her, "It's a little early for news. The home study visit was yesterday."

"I can't help it. I might have been reluctant to believe in you at first, but I'm all in now. I can't wait to hear that you're going to be Frankie's foster dad."

"Thank you, Tamara." He sounded so pleased.

"Hey, what's a friend for, right?"

"Right." He fell silent.

"Jace? You still there?"

"Yeah. Right here. And I do have something I really need to talk to you about."

Her heart was bouncing against the walls of her chest now. She took a slow breath and ordered it to calm the heck down. There was absolutely no reason for her to be nervous right now.

But she was.

She said, "Whatever it is, talk to me. Please."

And then he said, "Let me take you out. Tomorrow night. I'll pick you up at seven for dinner at The Association."

The fancy cattleman's club in Bronco Heights was pretty much legendary. The restaurant there served prime beef, and you couldn't just buy a membership, you had to be sponsored for the privilege of handing over the giant yearly dues.

She wanted to go. And not because it was where all the rich people hung out, but because she would be going with Jace. She wanted to *be* with him—and not only as his friend. She wanted—

Oh, please.

What was she thinking?

They were friends. Friends only.

She'd made that very clear to him and yet, here he was, trying to change the rules on her.

Her wildly beating heart echoed in her ears. Because this was a problem.

And she needed to fix it now.

"I just want to be clear, Jace. Are you asking me out?"

"I am, yes." The three little words curled around inside her, stirring up all sorts of feelings she didn't want to deal with. And he had more to say. "That's exactly what I'm doing. I'm asking you out to dinner with me tomorrow night."

"Oh, Jace. I, um… We're friends, remember? Friends only. We agreed." She felt terrible. She never

More to Love.
More to Explore.

With more to explore, we'd love to send you up to 4 BOOKS, absolutely FREE when you try the Harlequin Reader Service.

They say that "less is more" — but not when it comes to reading your favorite books!

We know that readers like you can't wait to open their newest book and settle down reading.

We feel the same way. That's why today, you can say "YES" to MORE of the great reading you love — absolutely FREE!

Try **Harlequin® Special Edition** and get 2 books featuring comfort and strength in the support of loved ones and enjoying the journey no matter what life throws your way.

Try **Harlequin® Heartwarming™ Larger-Print** and get 2 books featuring uplifting stories where the bonds of friendship, family and community unite.

Or TRY BOTH and get 2 books from each series!

Your free books are completely free, even the shipping! If you continue with your subscription, you can look forward to curated monthly shipments of brand-new books from your selected series, always at a discount off the cover price! Plus you can cancel any time.

So don't miss out, return your Free Books Claim Card today to get your Free books.

Pam Powers

Free Books Claim Card
Say "Yes" to More Books!

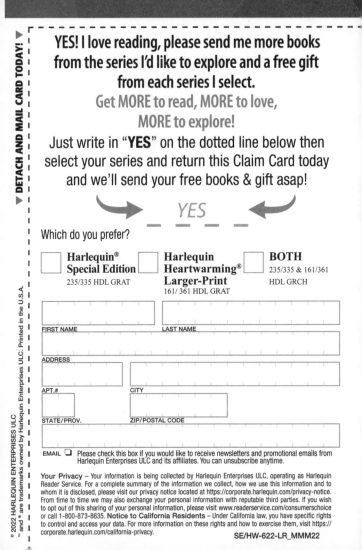

▼ DETACH AND MAIL CARD TODAY! ▼

YES! I love reading, please send me more books from the series I'd like to explore and a free gift from each series I select.

Get MORE to read, MORE to love, MORE to explore!

Just write in "**YES**" on the dotted line below then select your series and return this Claim Card today and we'll send your free books & gift asap!

→ _YES_ ←

Which do you prefer?

☐ **Harlequin®**
Special Edition
235/335 HDL GRAT

☐ **Harlequin**
Heartwarming®
Larger-Print
161/ 361 HDL GRAT

☐ **BOTH**
235/335 & 161/361
HDL GRCH

FIRST NAME

LAST NAME

ADDRESS

APT.#

CITY

STATE/PROV.

ZIP/POSTAL CODE

EMAIL ☐ Please check this box if you would like to receive newsletters and promotional emails from Harlequin Enterprises ULC and its affiliates. You can unsubscribe anytime.

should have kissed him. "Last night I, uh, gave you the wrong signal. I'm sorry. I really am."

The silence on his end went on way too long.

"Jace?"

"Uh, yeah. Still here. Friends only. I heard you."

"Please don't be—"

"Don't be what? Disappointed? Well, Tamara, I am disappointed. But you're right. Friends only is what we agreed. Sorry for stepping over the line. You have a good weekend." She heard a click and he was gone.

"Jace," she whispered to her empty living room.

Really, she'd done the right thing. And he'd known up front where she stood about the two of them. Friends only. That was all she could offer him. She had nothing to feel sorry about—well, except for the kiss she shouldn't have liked so much or even let happen, for that matter.

Oh, but she didn't feel sorry for kissing him. She had *loved* kissing him.

Right now, she only felt sorry for turning down his invitation to dinner. She felt like bursting into tears and then calling him back like some slightly deranged person who didn't know her own mind. Calling him back and begging him to take her to dinner, after all.

Slowly, she sank back to the sofa.

Was that it, then? Was it over and done between her and Jace?

No. No, of course not.

They were still friends. In a few days, she would reach out, ask him how he was doing, remind him that she was there for him, smooth over the awful awkwardness of just now.

It would be fine.

With a silly little moan, she grabbed a throw pillow and pressed it to her face. "I should have said yes, shouldn't I?" she whined into the pillow.

There was no answer. After all, she was home alone.

Chapter Six

Tamara had Saturday and Sunday off that week.

No way could she sit home Saturday night—too depressing, given that she could have been enjoying an evening out with Jace. She called Stephanie, but her friend already had plans with Geoff for the evening.

Tamara made more calls. Turned out one of the other nurses and a couple of the lab technicians were getting together. She tagged along—even though they were going to Doug's and she felt more than a little nervous she might run into Jace or one of his brothers there.

Didn't happen. She had a beer and shared a giant platter of Doug's famous chili cheese nachos and played several games of eight ball. When she went home at midnight, she couldn't decide whether she was relieved or let down that Jace had spent his Saturday night somewhere else.

Sunday wasn't so bad. She remembered that Jace volunteered round-the-clock at the firehouse from Sunday till Monday. It seemed unlikely he might decide to call her while on duty and she didn't want to bother him at work, anyway. She went grocery shopping, puttered around the house and binge-watched the latest season of *Bridgerton*.

Monday, she worked a long shift, during which she assisted at the births of two beautiful babies. By the time she got home, she was tired—too tired to pick up the phone and see how Jace might be doing. Tuesday went by pretty much the same way—he didn't call. And she couldn't quite make herself seize the initiative and call him.

By Wednesday, she'd begun to feel downright glum. Not to mention a complete wimp, too chicken to pick up the phone and reach out. She'd started to wonder if he might have decided she was simply too contradictory, insisting they were just friends, kissing him ardently—and then reminding him they were friends-only when he called to ask her out.

She could get whiplash thinking about her own behavior.

The thing to do was to call him, ask to see him and then make it very clear to him that she really liked him and didn't want to lose touch with him. Or if she was just too much of a coward to call, why not send a short text saying she missed him and would he meet her for a beer?

Keeping up a friendship was not rocket science. A woman had to reach out, to make her interest in the other person clear.

She failed to call him or text him all day Wednesday—or that evening for that matter.

Thursday morning during her first break, she went so far as to bring up his number on her phone. But somehow, she couldn't get herself to poke the little phone icon or even send him a text.

She sat there at the break table, shaking her head, staring down at the screen, mentally calling herself all kinds of chicken—a fainthearted shirker, a yellow-bellied scaredy-cat—when the phone rang in her hand.

She blinked down at it and read Jace Abernathy.

Gasping in surprise, she almost dropped the phone and ended up kind of bouncing it from hand to hand for a couple of seconds, before finally catching it.

"You okay, Tamara?" Ashana, from HR, stared at her through worried eyes.

"Fine, thanks. Really." She jumped from the chair. "I just need to get this." She was punching the green icon to accept the call as she speed walked for the door that led out to the courtyard. "Jace! Hi."

"Hey…" His voice trailed off. "Is this a bad time? You sound kind of—"

"No! No, really. It's a great time. Don't hang up. Just…hold on?"

"Uh. Sure."

She pushed through the door to the courtyard and went straight to a small bench with no one seated near it. "I'm on break," she explained. "I thought I would come outside where I won't disturb anyone in the lounge, you know?"

"Makes sense." He sounded kind of guarded.

She could hardly blame him. She'd turned down his dinner invitation and never quite managed to reach out and make sure he knew that she still wanted to help him with the Frankie situation any way she could, that she really did hope to remain his friend.

"Look, Tamara, if you don't want to hear from me—"

"What? Wait! No, no…" Her heart had started banging away in her chest, and her face felt so hot suddenly. She pressed her free hand to her cheek to cool it. Boy, was she blowing this. Coming off like a preteen who'd been raised in a cave and taught no social skills whatsoever. "I've, um, well, I've been meaning to call you."

"You have?"

"Yeah, I…" A small groan escaped her. "Truth?"

"Hit me with it."

"I've been trying all week to get up the *nerve* to call you."

A silence on his end. She heard him draw a slow breath.

She forged ahead. "But apparently, I'm a complete wuss, one of those people who can't even manage to call a guy and let him know that she, um, likes him a lot and doesn't want to lose contact."

"She doesn't, huh?"

"Okay, that sounded lame. Let me try again. Jace, *I* like you a lot and *I* don't want to lose contact with you. I do want to be your friend, and I still want to help out with Frankie in any way I can."

"You sure about that?" He was smiling. She could hear it in his voice.

"Yes, I am. Very, very sure."

"Well, I'm glad. Because I like you, too. And it just so happens I have news."

Her heart started racing all over again. "You do? Did that woman from Child and Family Services call?"

"Yes, she did. An hour ago, as a matter of fact."

"And…?"

"I'm going to be a foster dad."

"Omigosh!" she whisper-shouted. "That's amazing. When?"

"I pick up Frankie first thing tomorrow—I mean, I have to be there first thing. My mother, the expert, says I'll be there getting instructions and filling out forms, just generally jumping through all the hoops, for at least a few hours. Frankie and I will be lucky to get back to the Bonnie B by early afternoon."

For a moment, she couldn't speak. And then she realized that tears were sliding down her face. "Oh, Jace. I can hardly believe it. You did it." She fumbled in a pocket of her scrub pants for a tissue.

"Tamara? Are you okay?"

"I am. I'm great. It's just that I'm…" She dabbed at her leaking eyes. "Suddenly ridiculously emotional—in the best kind of way, I promise you." She laughed and swiped more tears away, not even caring that a couple of ward clerks were eyeing her apprehensively from across the courtyard. "What can I do to help?"

"What time are you off duty today?"

"Seven."

"So you should be at your house by seven fifteen or so?"

"That's about right."

"I've got to drive into town anyway this afternoon. Somehow, Roxy James and that guy at the TV station both knew before *I* did that I'm cleared to be Frankie's foster dad. I barely got off the line with the social worker before my phone was blowing up with calls for interviews, which I agreed to give them this afternoon. I was thinking I would grab some takeout and meet you at your house afterward?"

"Yes," she said without hesitation.

"We can catch up. I mean, it's been too long, right?"

"Yes, it has—and I'm putting in my request right now."

"Request for what?"

"I work tomorrow, but I want to drive out to the ranch as soon as my shift is over. I never thought I would see Frankie again. If it's all right with you, I want to welcome him home."

"It's more than all right. So I'll see you tonight and tomorrow, you'll come on out to the ranch."

"Yes, perfect." She sniffled with sheer happiness. "Wow, Jace. You did it. You really did it. I'm so happy for you."

Jace got into town at a little after three that day.

His visits to the *Bronco Bulletin* and KBTV took forever. Afterward, when he went to pick up the to-go order from his favorite barbecue place, they'd had some mix-up on his order and had to start over. A half an hour later, they finally handed him the food.

Tamara's RAV4 was already parked in her driveway when he got to her house. He was halfway up the front walk, a big bag of takeout in each hand, when she burst out the front door with a giant smile on her face.

Damn, she looked good, in a yellow sundress and white Vans, her dark hair loose on her shoulders.

"Sorry I'm a little late."

"Are you kidding? You're here and you brought dinner." She paused a few feet from him and sniffed the air. "Which smells delicious, by the way."

He wanted to drop the takeout bags right there on the walk and grab her in a hug.

But then he would only want to take it further, go in for a kiss. And he needed to quell that urge. After all, she'd said she only wanted friendship.

Did he believe her when she said that?

Nope. But a guy had to listen to what a woman actually said and behave accordingly. No jumping to his own conclusions based on wishful thinking and that glowing smile on her face when she came running out the door to greet him.

She wasn't ready to take it to the next level. Maybe she never would be. He could live with that.

For now, anyway.

Inside, she took the bags to the kitchen counter, put the food on plates and brought him a beer. They sat at the dinner table that marked off her kitchen from the living area. Harley slithered under the table, no doubt to be ready and waiting if either of them dropped a morsel of food.

"The ribs are amazing." Tamara waved one at him.

He sipped his beer. "Yeah. They have some issues with their take-out process, but nobody ever complains about the food."

"I saw you on KBTV again today," she said, then teased, "I think you're destined for stardom."

"Hardly. I'm hoping that's my last appearance. They wanted to come out to the ranch tomorrow and do a segment with Frankie."

"From the look on your face right now, I'm guessing you said no?"

"I did, yeah. I'm grateful to the station. I wouldn't be picking Frankie up tomorrow if not for the opportunity they gave me to tell the world what Melissa wanted for her baby. But tomorrow's an important day. It's Frankie's first day with me. The last thing I want is to put it on TV."

"I agree." She wiped her hands on her napkin and then reached over to clasp his arm. He wished she would leave that soft hand of hers right there, touching him, skin to skin, forever. "Some things are private," she said as she held his gaze with those gorgeous brown eyes of hers. "I was only teasing about the stardom thing."

"I know."

"And it's a lot to deal with, your first day as a dad. It's going to be wonderful but also stressful—and the priority has to be Frankie."

"Yeah, that's how I feel, too."

After they finished eating, they cleared off the table together and then settled on her sofa. Harley jumped right up and sprawled out on the cushion between them.

"So I have news," she said. "I managed to get the afternoon off tomorrow."

He tried not to stare at her mouth. It was an effort. Damn. He wanted to kiss her, though he knew no kissing would happen tonight or anytime in the near future, if at all—and what were they talking about?

Right. She was getting off work early. "So you'll come out to the Bonnie B in the afternoon, then?"

"If that works for you."

"You bet it does. I should be there with Frankie by one or so, I hope—and just so you're forewarned, my mom will be at the cabin, too. And probably my dad and possibly everyone else in the family."

Her gaze slid away. "So, then maybe you've got all the help you need for tomorrow."

"What? No way. Frankie and I will be expecting you. Don't let us down."

That brought back her soft smile. "Well, okay, then. I'll be there." She made a thoughtful sound. "I envy you your big family, the way everyone pitches in whenever they're needed."

He might have joked that a big family had its downside, what with everyone knowing everyone else's business and not the least reluctant to share their opinions. But her beautiful face had a wistful look, and that had him reminding himself that he really had hit the jackpot familywise. "I'm a lucky man, all right."

"Text me if there's any last-minute baby gear you need, and I'll pick it up before I leave."

"Thanks. I mean, I think I'm all set, but you never know." He watched her slim hand as she petted Harley in long, slow strokes. The cat purred with contentment, his golden eyes low and lazy. Jace let his gaze wander upward. When he met her eyes, she seemed anxious. She'd caught her lower lip between her pretty white teeth. "Jace, I…"

He resisted the need to reach for her, to pull her close, to promise her that whatever was bothering her, he would make it right. "Tamara, just go ahead. Say it, whatever it is."

"You're going to think I don't know my own mind."

"No."

"Yeah. And you *should* think I don't know my own mind, because, boy, am I giving you mixed signals or what?"

"It's okay."

"No, it's not. After my last relationship crashed and burned, I swore to myself I would just stay away from men, not go out, not get anything going, you know? Not for a while, anyway. And I meant what I said the other night when you called to ask me out. I really did plan to keep it friends-only with us. But I…" She blew out a hard breath. "Well, the truth is, I've missed you so much and I really care for you and… Sheesh." She buried her head in her hands. Harley got up, stretched and jumped down from between them. Tamara groaned. "I'm making a complete mess of this."

"No, you're not." He waited until she finally dropped her hands into her lap and looked at him again. "Just talk to me, Tamara. I really am listening."

"I was wrong, that's all."

"About...?"

"You and me being just friends."

He'd been trying not to get his hopes up. But he liked where she was going with this. He liked it a lot.

With effort, he kept his mouth shut and waited for her to continue.

And she did. "Jace, I was lying to myself. And I was a coward. And the truth is I *am* attracted to you, and I also think the world of you, and if I could go back and do last Friday night over, I would say, 'Yes, Jace. I would love to go out to dinner with you'— and not just as friends, if you know what I mean."

He sat absolutely still. Because he wanted to grab her, haul her close and cover her sweet mouth with his.

But she'd come a long way since last Friday night, and he didn't want to spook her. He definitely didn't want to lose any of the ground he'd gained with her.

She groaned again. "Say something. Please!"

"Tamara, will you go out to dinner with me?"

The sweetest smile trembled across her lips. "I will, yes."

"Soon."

"Yes."

He needed to lock this in before she could get cold

feet and change her mind. "Friday night, a week from tomorrow, at The Association."

"Yes."

He really liked the sound of that word on her lips. "I'm going to need to get a sitter." That sounded amazing all by itself.

"Yes, you will." Those dark eyes were shining bright.

"Tamara…"

"Hmm?" She swayed toward him, her soft mouth tipped up.

"I don't want to do anything you're not ready for…"

She grinned then. "Good idea. Because I'm not ready for a lot of things."

"Fair enough."

"But I am ready for…"

"Say it."

Her grin got wider. "A kiss, Jace."

His arms ached to hold her. "You're sure?"

She whispered, "Oh, yeah."

And that did it. He reached out, gathered her in and lowered his mouth to hers.

She sighed. He drank in that tender, perfect sound as she opened to him.

"Jace…" She murmured his name against his lips, and he pulled her even closer, kissed her a little deeper—but carefully, too. He wasn't going to rush this.

Yeah, she was strong and self-sufficient, but she was cautious, too. More than one jerk had hurt her. He needed to keep things at a pace that wouldn't spook her.

So he took his time, stroking her silky hair and kissing her some more—short, soft kisses, and then deeper, longer kisses.

He scooted up against the armrest, and she leaned back across his lap, kicked off her shoes and stretched out along the cushions.

"I missed you," she said. "I really did."

"I'm here now." He breathed in the fresh scent of her hair—like apples and lemons, both sweet and tart.

Her breath came a little faster as he slipped a finger slowly along the silky skin of her throat. He was more than a little tempted to keep going, to trail his touch lower, to curve his hand around the soft swell of her breast.

But he didn't. Some things demanded restraint. Some things couldn't be rushed.

He lifted his head. Staring down at her, he memorized the dreamy look in her eyes, the just-kissed flush on her cheeks.

They remained right there on the sofa for the longest time. They talked about tomorrow. He said how much it meant to him to have made the first big step toward keeping his promise to Melissa. Now, he felt increasingly certain that Frankie would grow up calling him Dad.

It was almost ten when she walked him to the door.

They shared one more kiss, there at the door, their arms wrapped around each other.

And then she was scooping Harley into her arms before pulling the door wide.

Jace went out into the summer night. Overhead, the dark bowl of the sky glittered with a million stars. Turning, he walked backward all the way down her front walk, so that he could see her standing there in the glow of the porch light, barefoot in a yellow dress, her black cat cradled in her arms.

Tamara had the windows down, and she could hear the baby wailing inside the cabin when she stopped her RAV4 a few yards from the porch.

Grabbing her shoulder bag and the baby gift she'd found at a cute little boutique on Commercial Street before she'd headed out of town, she ran up the steps and knocked.

The door swung wide to reveal Jace with a screaming Frankie cradled in his arms. "Thank God you're here." His eyes were wild, and his thick chestnut hair looked like he'd been raking his fingers through it.

She craned her head to see behind him. It appeared that he and Frankie were all alone. "Where is everyone?"

"I sent them away." He rocked the unhappy infant from side to side, but Frankie kept on wailing. "They all had advice. Everybody knew what I was doing wrong." He kissed Frankie's angry little face. "They weren't helping," he grumbled. "So I told them to leave."

She set her purse and the brightly wrapped baby gift on the table by the door. "Shall I take him?"

"Yes, please." He gently handed over the yowling bundle. "I think I might have lost hearing in my left ear."

"You'll be fine."

"Easy for you to say."

She put the baby on her shoulder. He continued to cry. She started walking, making a circuit of the main room, swaying from side to side as she went, gently patting his back. "You've fed him, I'm guessing?"

Jace nodded as Frankie sobbed. "Fed him a half hour ago. Tried again five minutes ago. He didn't want it. And he doesn't need a diaper change."

She pressed her palm to Frankie's forehead as he screamed his little lungs out. "No fever. Maybe gas?"

"I burped him. I don't think it's that."

They continued down the list of all the possible reasons the poor little guy was so unhappy. Tamara positioned him along her arm to soothe possible colic. It didn't help. She took him into Jace's room, put him on the bed, took off everything but his diaper and gently massaged his chest, arms and kicking legs. That seemed to soothe him a little, but then he started right in crying again.

"Is his car seat still in your truck?" she asked as she finished dressing him and gathered him close once more.

Jace stood in the bedroom doorway, big shoulders slumped. "Yeah."

"We may have to drive him around for a while. That works on a lot of babies. But before we try that, does he have a pacifier?"

"No. My mom's not a fan. He had one when we picked him up, but she took it. I think she tossed it in the trash."

Tamara rubbed Frankie's little back and whispered softly, "Shh, now. You're okay, everything is okay," as she rocked him again. "That may be our problem. He's probably missing his pacifier. There's one attached to the ribbon on the package I brought for him."

The baby let out an especially loud wail, so she tried to lay him in the colic-relieving position along her arm again. He kept right on sobbing.

Still slouching in the doorway, Jace rubbed the back of his neck. He probably had a headache. She was certainly getting one. "But aren't pacifiers bad for a baby?" he asked.

"Some people think so." Frankie let out a loud, angry cry. She put him on her shoulder again and spoke louder to be heard over his cries. "Really, though, a pacifier can be so helpful for a little one to learn to self soothe. Frankie's had a stressful day. He's in a strange place, and from what you just said, I'm guessing he's been using a pacifier with his former foster family. I'm thinking that taking it away right now might not be the wisest choice."

Jace gave her a slow nod. "Where's the one you brought?"

"By the front door. It's new and will need to be sterilized. To do that, boil about a quart of water. Put the pacifier in and keep the water boiling for five minutes. Be careful you don't let it touch the side of the pan. That would damage it. Once it's clean, take it by the handle. Shake it to get the water out and to cool it a bit."

"Will do." He left her.

While he was gone, Frankie wet his diaper.

But Jace had thought of everything. He had a changing area set up right there in his bedroom, along with a bassinet, so Frankie could sleep in Jace's room for now.

She changed the diaper and then tried swaddling the little guy to settle him down.

Swaddling worked no better than anything else had. She was really hoping the pacifier would do the trick. And just for the heck of it, she carried him into the ensuite bathroom, washed her pinky, cradled him on the other arm and let him suck on her finger.

The silence when he latched on with a big, relieved sigh?

Heaven.

He watched her in that dazed way new babies have.

"What did you do?" Jace asked in a hushed, amazed whisper from the doorway to his bedroom. He dangled the pacifier by its handle.

She gave him a one-shouldered shrug and then focused on Frankie again. He looked like an angel now, sucking away, completely blissed out. "Some things are more alike than you'd think—for instance, a pinky finger and a pacifier. For Frankie's purposes, they're pretty much the same thing." She signaled Jace forward with a tip of her chin. "Bring that here."

Frankie let out a small cry of outrage when she popped her finger from his mouth, but when she gave him the pacifier instead, he latched right on and started sucking away.

"Here." She offered Jace the baby. "Hold your little boy."

Jace took him in his arms. "Look at you," he said to the baby. "Feeling better?"

With a contented sigh, Frankie let his eyes drift shut.

Tamara grinned at Jace in the bathroom mirror. "Hear that? It's called silence."

"And it is amazing." They were both whispering.

Tamara caught a flash of movement in the corner

of her eye. She turned to see both Bailey and Luna sitting at attention in the doorway to the bathroom. "Where did you guys come from?"

Bailey let out a hopeful whine, and Luna beat her tail against the hardwood floor.

Jace chuckled softly. "I think Frankie's crying really got to them. They're both pretty sensitive, and they hate when someone's suffering. While he was wailing, they followed me around for a while, staring up at me, begging me with their big eyes to help the baby. They stuck with me for a bit after I sent my mom and the rest of the family away.

"But there came a point where they just couldn't take it. They disappeared before you arrived—into the laundry room maybe, or even upstairs. I was so busy trying to calm this guy down, I didn't notice where they went."

"Aw, girls," Tamara said. "It's okay now." She went to them, dropping to a crouch to give them some attention. When she rose again, she clicked her tongue. "Come on. Let's get out of the doorway." The dogs followed her into the bedroom. Jace did, too. Tamara nodded at the bundle in his arms. "He has to be exhausted."

"No doubt."

"He should sleep for a while now."

"I'll put him in the bassinet in a little while. But right this minute, I just want to hold him." Jace sat on the edge of the bed and stared down at the baby as though he held a miracle in his big arms.

Because he did.

"Did you ever doubt you would get to this point?" Tamara asked.

"Every damn day since I promised his mom I would bring him home."

"And yet here you are, Frankie's foster dad."

"Yeah." He glanced up and their gazes locked. Something sweet and tender passed between them.

She asked softly, "Feels good, huh?"

"Ten minutes ago, no. I felt like the worst excuse for a dad on the planet."

"But now?"

"Right now, it's like I've won the lottery, climbed the highest mountain, kept a promise I knew deep down I couldn't keep. I feel like this little guy and me, we're meant to become a family."

She nodded. "You look good together, though I had my doubts you would manage it."

"I know you did."

"But not anymore, Jace. You're on your way to adopting him." A lovely, warm shiver skittered up the backs of her knees as he continued to stare into her eyes with a look both heated and full of promise.

"Thank you," he said. "You're a miracle worker."

She almost went to him, sat down beside him, leaned her head on his broad shoulder, and let herself imagine for a few brief, beautiful moments that they were really in this together, committed as a team to making a home for little Frankie.

But instead, she remained right where she was. She reminded herself yet again that she and Jace were friends—and after last night, maybe a little bit more than friends. But that was all. She would not go jumping to dangerous conclusions.

"Hey." She kept her voice light, cheerful. "I know all the baby-soothing secrets." She laughed, but quietly, so as not to disturb the little boy snoozing in his arms. "You know the ones I mean—the ones most everybody who ever had a child has had to learn."

"I consider you my best weapon in the battle to be a decent dad."

Did her heart melt just a little all over again when he said that?

Well, why shouldn't it?

Last night they'd grown closer. And this, right now, was a great moment in the middle of an important day for him and Frankie.

Of course, she felt good about it. "Happy to help. I do mean that. Right now, the girls and I will go on into the other room. I think you and Frankie could use a little alone time." She clicked her tongue.

Luna and Bailey fell in step behind her.

Chapter Seven

Jace was still back in the bedroom with Frankie when someone tapped on the front door.

It was Jace's mom, carrying a big casserole dish covered in foil. "Tamara!" Bonnie seemed genuinely delighted to see her. "I thought that was your SUV."

"Hey. Just came by to help out." She ushered Bonnie in and quietly shut the door.

"I'm going to put this in the fridge," Bonnie said. "It's beef and noodles. Easy to heat up when you're too busy to do much more than stick something in the microwave."

"Jace will appreciate that."

Bonnie headed for the arch to the kitchen area and returned a minute later. "I take it Jace is with the baby?"

"Yeah, he's taking a few minutes, just the two of them."

Bonnie beamed. "He's going to make a wonderful dad—and I have to say, I was so relieved when I saw you drive up. I hated to leave him alone with the little guy so upset, but he insisted."

"It was touch and go when I got here, but we managed to settle Frankie down."

Bonnie perched on the leather easy chair and gestured toward the sofa. "Sit with me."

Tamara hesitated. "I'm going to assume that if you want coffee or anything, you know where to get it."

Bonnie chuckled. "Yes, I do." Tamara sat on the sofa and Bonnie asked, "So I'm guessing that Frankie finally wore himself out?"

"Not exactly. We tried everything to calm him down. A pacifier finally did the trick."

Bonnie made a face. "I confess. When we picked Frankie up, I got rid of the one the foster mom had stuck in his mouth. I've never approved of them."

"Jace told me."

Bonnie tipped her head to the side, frowning slightly. "But…you believe otherwise?"

"I believe that a pacifier is like so many things. Good in moderation. Especially for a new baby in a whole new place, with all new people around him. A pacifier can really soothe a little one in a situation like this one."

"Well." Now Bonnie was nodding. "I do see your point. And you are the expert."

Somehow, Tamara hadn't expected Jace's strong-minded mom to be so easily convinced. "*Expert* might be too strong a word."

"But you specialize in new moms and babies."

"Yes, I do."

"Then if you're not an expert, I don't know who is."

"Well, thank you. And yes, when it comes to new babies, I've had a lot of experience."

"Exactly."

"Mom." Jace, a baby monitor in his hand, walked into the living room.

Bonnie rose. "I just came by to drop off my beef noodle casserole for you."

"Thanks."

"So, then, you've put him to bed?"

"Yep." Jace came fully into the room, and his mother met him halfway. "Now I'm going to enjoy the peace and quiet while it lasts."

"An excellent plan." Bonnie turned a big smile on Tamara. "Well, I'm off. Tamara, again, I am so glad to see you here." Two seconds later, she was out the door.

Jace shut it behind her. "What did she say to you?"

"She called me an expert."

"That's a problem?"

"No. Of course not. She was very sweet and flattering."

"Sweet." He stuck his hands in his pockets, his powerful shoulders hunching a little with the movement. "That's a word I wouldn't generally use when describing my mom. Most people call her things like 'admirable,' 'determined' and 'strong-minded.'"

"So, then why is she so sweet to me?"

"Well, because she likes you?"

"Jace, you just answered my question with a question."

"I know. Let me put it this way. She clearly admires you and appreciates that you're helping out with Frankie."

"But isn't it more common for a guy's mom to be cautious when her son starts spending time with someone new?" She'd met Eric's mom once. The woman had been cool and watchful.

"Tamara, you need to face it."

That didn't sound good. "I do?"

Now he was grinning. He crossed the distance between them, set the baby monitor on the coffee table and sat down beside her, stirring the air a little, tempting her with his wonderful, woodsy scent. "You're smart and beautiful and you care about people. My mother *likes* you." He rested his arm along the back of the sofa. "*I* like you. A lot."

"Smart and beautiful, huh?"

"Oh, yeah." He was so close and he smelled so good. When his warm lips met hers, she was smiling.

"How about some beef and noodles?" he asked a while later. By then, her mouth felt tender and swollen from kissing him, and all she wanted was to sit there and kiss him some more.

Too bad her stomach, which she hadn't fed since six thirty that morning, chose that moment to growl.

"I believe that's a yes." He took her hand and pulled her to her feet.

The casserole was still warm from Bonnie's oven. Tamara had two helpings.

When Frankie woke an hour later, Jace fed him and changed him. For a while, they hung out in the living area, the three of them and the dogs. Tamara and Jace took turns holding the baby.

By eight that night, Frankie was out like a light. Jace put him to bed and rejoined Tamara in the main room. They streamed a movie with the volume turned low so as not to wake Frankie, and then hardly glanced at the flatscreen over the fireplace. Instead, they whispered together and shared a long string of sweet kisses.

At a little after ten, she got up to go. He tried to talk her into staying even later.

"Can't. I traded the second half of my shift today for a full shift tomorrow. And this week, I'm working Sunday, too."

At the door, he took her in his arms. "I'm working Sunday to Monday."

"Right. At the fire station."

"I'm really hoping I can see you before then."

"Well, I could stop by after work tomorrow."

"Yes! I'll feed you." He guided a swatch of her hair behind her ear. His touch felt so good, his fingertips a little rough but just right. Bending closer, he nuzzled her ear and whispered, "Be warned. Tomorrow night, I'll be a bad influence. I'm going to try to convince you to stay late."

"I can't stay past ten—and I hope you have someone to watch Frankie during your shift at the station."

"It's handled. Stacy and my mom will take turns with him. Then, this coming week, we're going to start interviewing for a regular nanny. The family will help, but it's not fair to count on them all the time."

"Makes sense."

He touched the lines that suddenly formed between her eyebrows. "You're frowning. Why?"

"Well, a good nanny can be expensive."

He smirked. "You're worried I can't afford a nanny?"

"No. I didn't say that."

"But you thought it."

"Sorry. Just being practical."

"Well, you can stop worrying. I may look like your average cowboy and volunteer firefighter—and I am. But I'm also an Abernathy. We all have shares in the profits here on the ranch, plus an inheritance that we got control of in our twenties. And both my dad and mom made sure we all learned early how to manage what we have. Please don't worry, Tamara. I can afford to pay a nanny."

She felt a little bit silly. "I guess I should have figured that out for myself."

"Never hurts to ask—and I like that you're looking out for me." He tipped up her chin with a finger. "Damn. I really don't want you to go."

She didn't want to go, either. Especially not when his lips met hers and she sank into another perfect kiss.

That time, when he lifted his head, she gave his broad chest a gentle push. "Good night, Jace."

He pretended to scowl. "You sound like you mean business."

"I do. Open the door. Say goodbye."

He stood on the porch and watched her drive away.

At home in her bed, with Harley curled up and purring beside her, she spent way too much of the time she should have been sleeping replaying every kiss she and Jace had shared, wishing there could have been more of them—and knowing there would be.

For a woman who'd insisted just a week ago that she and Jace had to keep it friends-only, she'd definitely changed her tune. She felt equal parts thrilled and terrified about that.

Should she be more cautious?

Probably.

She ought to lay out some ground rules, insist

that she really couldn't be rushing to his side every chance she got.

Except…

She wanted to be with him. So much. She was done trying to play it cool.

Her Saturday shift at Bronco Valley Hospital started out crappy. A first-time mom had a difficult birth. The new mom's ob-gyn ended up performing an emergency C-section, at which Tamara assisted.

Both the mom and the baby pulled through, but it was touch and go there for a while. At one point, they couldn't get a heartbeat on the child.

By the end, though, the infant girl was breathing normally and cradled in her mother's loving arms.

Tamara got a break at eleven thirty. She went on over to the cafeteria for lunch. Eric was there with Elise.

The sight of them together didn't feel like a spike through her heart the way it had during those first weeks after she'd caught him in one of the supply closets making Elise moan his name. Tamara felt glad about that. She was definitely over the guy.

Everything about Eric Pearce seemed phony to her now. His conservatively cut, perfectly styled hair, his smarmy smiles. The way he still winked at her occasionally—what was that about? The man was a douche canoe, pure and simple.

He was a good doctor, though, she reminded herself. Everyone said so.

But still. Why couldn't he and Elise just ride off into the sunset together? She would be perfectly happy if she never had to see either of them again.

After lunch, it seemed like there was one crisis after another.

When she left the hospital, it was past seven. She should probably call Jace and beg off on her visit to the ranch, say she was tired, that it had been a long day.

But no. She really wanted to see him, to hear about his day, to share a few kisses and hold Frankie in her arms.

Was this getting out of hand?

She decided not to think about that. Instead, she went home, hugged and fed her cat and took a quick shower.

Jace was waiting on the front porch when she pulled up in front of his cabin. He had the baby monitor on the little table beside his chair. She ran up the steps and into his waiting arms.

Inside, he shared all the details of his day with Frankie.

"I swear he knows me already," Jace claimed. "Sometimes when he looks up at me, I feel like we're a team, you know? But last night after you left, he woke up. He cried. Even the pacifier didn't seem to help. I was getting worried—and then he filled his diaper."

She laughed. "All better?"

"Pretty much. I changed him and he went right back to sleep. Not me, though. I was still tied in knots from trying to stay calm while he cried his little heart out."

She reached up and pressed her palm against his lean cheek. "You do look tired."

"I think *haggard* is the word."

"You need to learn to sleep when he sleeps."

"I'll work on that. It'll be an adjustment."

She grabbed the collar of his shirt and pulled him down for a quick, hard kiss. "Welcome to fatherhood."

They settled on the sofa and streamed a couple episodes of *Reacher* that they didn't really watch. She left at ten thirty.

On shift at five the next morning, she dragged through the day.

Stephanie teased her. "You've been staying up late."

"All nights are late when you start work at five a.m."

Her friend wasn't buying that. "I'm going to make a bold assumption and say you've been spending your evenings with a certain handsome cowboy and his foster son."

"I'll never tell."

"You don't have to tell. You look wiped out but very happy." Stephanie moved in close and whispered, "You never looked this happy when you were seeing the cheater."

Tamara only smiled. After all, her friend was right. She had a feeling of rightness with Jace. He excited her and she liked him so much. Looking back now, she saw that things had never been right with Eric. There was always a distance between them, somehow. She'd never felt close to him, really.

And that made her sad—that she'd been so gullible about him, that she hadn't seen through him right away.

As for Jace—well, there was no denying that he rang all her bells. He was kind and he cared about other people, about doing the right thing. His kisses thrilled her.

But she couldn't stop asking herself if she should trust her own judgment when it came to men. Her dad had left when she was small. And her mom, seeking wealth and security, had moved from one man to another.

Yes, she wanted a good marriage with someone she could love and count on. She wanted kids, and she wanted to give those kids the kind of childhood she herself had never known.

But what made her think she had it in her to choose the right man? Her track record with relationships sucked.

Stephanie leaned close again. "You know I like Jace. And tired but happy is a really good look on you."

"Yeah?"

"Absolutely. Take my advice. Don't let the losers get you down."

When her shift ended, Tamara was tempted to drive out to the ranch. Maybe Jace's mom and sister could use a break from taking care of Frankie.

But no.

Really. She had her own life and she needed to spend a little time at home.

It was a nice evening. She cooked herself dinner, did the laundry and read an exciting romantic Western, one where the heroine dressed up as a boy and joined a cattle drive.

Jace called from the fire station at nine. The mere sound of his voice made her feel warm all over. He could only talk for a moment. "Just wanted to let you know I miss you," he said and she melted inside.

Oh, yeah. She was falling. No doubt about it. Falling harder and faster than she ever had before.

When they said goodbye, she ached to call him right back again—but she didn't.

In the first dark hours of the morning, she woke to the sound of sirens in the distance. She bolted upright in bed and cried, "Jace!"

Was that him, then? Was he out on a call? She

flopped back to her pillow and said a silent prayer that he would be all right, that no one had been hurt, that everyone would be okay.

Harley got up, turned in a circle next to her and flopped back down close to her side. As usual, he was purring. The sound comforted her. But still, it took her a while to drift back to sleep.

At 7:30 a.m. she was sitting at her kitchen table thinking about getting the coffee started when her phone rang. It was Jace.

She tapped the talk icon and put the phone to her ear. "I heard sirens last night. Are you okay?"

"I'm fine. Just tired." His voice was flat.

"You don't sound fine, Jace."

"Tamara, you don't need to hear about it."

"Tell me."

He drew a weary-sounding breath. "An old man on oxygen decided he needed a smoke."

"Oh, no!"

"Yeah. Blew up his trailer. He didn't make it."

"I'm so sorry. And I hate to ask…"

"Go ahead."

"Was anyone else hurt?"

"No. Just the old man. Did some serious damage to the trailers on either side of his, but no one else got caught in the explosion. That's something at least, right?"

"It is and I'm glad to hear it. But still…" She had no idea how to finish that sentence. "You okay?"

"I've been better—and I really want to see you."

"Are you still at the station?"

"I'm on my way home. I was thinking that I might swing by your house for a few minutes. I need to get back, though. Stacy's been at my place all night, but I—"

"Go on home, Jace. I'm off today. I'll be at your cabin in half an hour."

Jace was watching at the window when Tamara arrived. Just the sight of her jumping out of that little SUV in snug jeans and a turquoise T-shirt made him smile for the first time since he and the full crew— fire engine, ambulance and police cruiser—arrived at that trailer park last night.

She ran up the steps. He pulled open the door and she threw herself on him, her slim arms curling tight around his neck. "Oh, Jace. I hope you're all right."

"I am now." He turned her and backed her up against the door until the latch clicked shut. Then he turned the lock.

"I'm so sorry about that old man," she whispered against his lips.

"I need you closer," he said.

"Anything you need…" With a little jump, she wrapped her legs around him, too.

He buried his nose in the crook of her neck—until she grabbed a fistful of his hair, yanked his head up and peppered his face with quick, eager kisses.

"How's Frankie?" she asked, pressing those sweet lips to his cheek first, then his chin and then the center of his forehead.

"Frankie's fine. Sound asleep."

She kissed him three more times—at his temple, his jawline and then on the other cheek.

"Good to see you, too," he said, and meant it.

Framing his face between her hands, she held him there, her gaze tracking from his eyes to his mouth and back to his eyes again, as though searching for clues to his mental well-being. "Are you sure you're all right?"

"I am, yeah." He took her mouth again, spearing his tongue in, tasting her deeply as he turned around again and headed for the sofa. When he got there, he sat with her straddling his lap.

They kissed some more, endless kisses interspersed with sighs and those tiny sounds she made—eager, happy sounds, like kissing him was everything. Like she could kiss him and kiss him and never, ever stop.

He understood her eagerness. After all, he felt the same about kissing her. And he wanted her. Bad. He ached to get closer.

But when she started unbuttoning his shirt, he caught her slim hands.

"What?" She looked up at him, her eyes soft, misty, her mouth swollen from all the kissing.

Yeah, he wanted her—all of her. But he didn't want to rush her. "Tamara, are you sure?"

She caught that plump lower lip between her teeth and nodded. "Yes, I am. At this moment, I am absolutely sure. And that surprises me. I'm usually more cautious."

That made him grin. "No kidding."

She almost smiled, but then she said very seriously, "I know I will be more guarded again later. But right now, I don't want to stop. Right now, I can see past all my fears and doubts and worries. Right now, I trust you. I really do. And I want you, Jace. So much."

Should he hold back, give her more time before taking this big step?

Probably.

But she'd just said yes. And that look in her eyes? It told him she wanted him as much as he longed for her.

Reaching around her, he grabbed the baby monitor from the coffee table. "Hold this."

She took it and then let out a squeak of surprise when he swept to his feet with her in his arms. "Jace! What are you doing?"

He dropped a kiss on the tip of her adorable nose. "Well, Frankie's in my room and the only bed in his room is a crib, so I'm taking you to my new guest room upstairs."

She curled an arm around his neck and nuzzled his throat. "I, um…"

"Just say it."

"There are a couple of things we should talk about."

"I'm listening."

She pulled back and asked, "Do you want to… put me down?"

He could stand there holding her forever. "Only if you want me to."

"Okay, then. Ahem." She rested her free hand over his heart. "If I go upstairs with you, I will want us to be…exclusive."

He didn't have to think twice about that. "Of course, Tamara. There's nobody else. And there won't be."

She drew a slow breath. "Okay, then. And also, I'm on the pill, but I believe in being safe on all fronts."

He caught her earlobe between his teeth and worried it gently, bringing a tiny moan from her as he whispered, "I completely agree. And that's why I not only moved the guest bed up there, but I also put condoms in the bedside drawer."

"Smooth," she replied with a grin.

"More like hopeful." He caught that beautiful mouth of hers again.

She kissed him back eagerly. For several minutes, he stood there between the sofa and coffee table, holding her high in his arms, kissing her endlessly.

But then, from over by the fireplace, Luna let out a questioning whine. He glanced that way. Both dogs were stretched out on the rug, heads up, watching them hopefully.

"Stay," he instructed.

Luna whined again, but both she and Bailey lowered their heads to their paws.

Stepping sideways to get out from behind the coffee table, Jace headed for the stairs.

Chapter Eight

At the top of the stairs, he went down the short hall to the room with the bed in it. When they got there at last, he carefully lowered her feet to the rug.

She looked around, taking in the queen-size bed, the black-and-white plaid bedding, the rustic bedroom furniture. "This is nice."

"Here. Let me have that." He took the monitor from her, set it on the bedside table and reached for her again.

She swayed toward him, softly sighing, filling his arms and all of his senses. He kissed her, another long, sweet kiss.

In the warm morning light slanting in the room's one window, they began to undress each other.

It seemed almost impossible that he was here with

her, holding her, slowly unwrapping her, revealing all her soft, perfect curves and secret places. They fell across the bed together, arms around each other, laughing, whispering tender encouragements. Her scent of apples and lemons surrounded him. She moaned eagerly as he caressed her, as he kissed his way over her pretty chin, along the silky length of her throat and then lower.

He wrapped his hand around the white swell of her breast and then covered it with his eager mouth.

She speared her fingers into his hair, pulling him closer, sighing his name. "Jace…"

The ugliness and pain of what had happened while he was on duty a few hours before, of a life so needlessly snuffed out, all that faded away, became a faint shadow far in the distance. Because here, in the morning light, with Tamara in his arms, there was no room for pain or loss.

There was only pleasure. Only goodness and the joy of having her close.

Her soft cries, her urgent pleas—they were exactly what he needed to remind him that life was a gift. That you did what you could to make things right, but sometimes it didn't matter what you did. Sometimes fate laughed at all your puny efforts. Sometimes, the darkness won.

And even knowing that, you had to go on, to help where you could, to fight the good fight—and not let the horrible things people did to themselves steal all the joy away.

Because when the right woman finally came along, a man needed to be open to her. He couldn't hold back. He had to reach for her with both hands, to kiss every inch of her, to show her that she mattered, that she was everything to him.

And now, on this suddenly perfect July morning, he did just that. Slowly, he kissed his way down the center of her body, between her breasts and lower. When he reached her thighs, he guided them to open wide.

Settling himself between them, he took his time kissing her in that most intimate place, using his tongue, stroking her with his fingers, as she cradled his head between her hands and begged him not to stop.

And he didn't stop. Not until she tossed her head wildly on the pillow, not until she cried out his name. Not until he felt her pulsing in release against his tongue.

For a while after that, his head cradled on the lower curve of her belly, they were still. He let himself enjoy the feel of her, right there with him, skin to skin. All his senses felt amplified. He paid careful attention to the sound of her breathing as it slowly settled from frantic and hungry to easy and slow.

"Oh, my." The two words escaped her lips in a whisper so faint, he hardly heard them.

Lifting his head a little, he looked up at her.

She had one arm thrown over her eyes, but he could see her mouth and she was smiling. With her other arm, she reached down to him. "Jace…"

"Right here." He scooted up beside her and gathered her close.

He needed to touch her some more, needed to have his hands all over her. So he stroked her tangled hair. He ran a lazy finger down the satin skin of her arm and back up again. Easing his hand around the nape of her neck, he brought her mouth closer and claimed it.

She made a sound—still eager, still ready for more. As she kissed him back, her fingers strayed down between them.

He groaned when her hand closed around his aching hardness. "Tamara…"

"Hmm?"

"You're going to be the death of me."

"Sorry," she said in a tone that let him know she wasn't sorry in the least.

A rough chuckle escaped him. "It wasn't a complaint."

Her lips brushed his cheek as she whispered, "About those condoms you said you had…"

He turned his head to capture her mouth in a kiss that started out light and teasing but quickly turned desperate and smoking hot. Flinging out an arm toward the night table, he fumbled for the drawer, got it open and took out a condom.

She asked, "Let me?"

He laid the pouch in her hand. Pushing him onto his back, she removed the foil wrapper and rolled the condom down over him.

He stared up at her, hardly daring to believe that this was happening, that he'd not only finally found this extraordinary woman, but that somehow, here she was, in bed with him.

He reached for her.

She came down to him and stretched out beside him. He rolled her carefully beneath him and covered her sweet mouth with his.

Easing a knee between her legs, he urged her to open again. She did, gazing up at him. Her pupils were blown, her mouth lush and deep red from so many kisses. She stared right into his eyes as he slid into her wet heat, gritting his teeth as he tried to go slow.

She was small and tight. He took care not to hurt her. He only hoped to make her feel the way he felt— like there was no other place in the world he would rather be than right here, in the morning light, naked in her arms.

"Jace," she said. "Oh, yes…"

He kissed her. She lifted her legs and wrapped them around him, tipping herself up to him, offering herself completely as he filled her all the way.

"I'm wild for you, Tamara. I've never known anyone like you."

Reaching up, she touched his lips with the tips of her fingers. "Jace…" A pleasured sound escaped her, a soft, needy little cry. She lifted her hips higher as she rocked against him.

Bringing her with him, he rolled to his side. She hooked one leg across his hip, and they moved together, deeper, closer. Fast and hard, then slower, sweeter…

It felt so good. He wanted it to last forever, but he feared that any second now, he would lose all control.

Again, he claimed the top position. Lifting up on his forearms, he took the lead. Tangling his fingers in her hair, he stroked into her until she cried out his name on a ragged breath. It was heaven, to feel her unraveling, coming undone, her body pulsing around him.

Chasing his own finish now, he tumbled over the edge right after her. Stars exploded behind his eyes as he let the pleasure take him, lifting him high, sending him flying.

Slowly, he drifted back down to earth. "Tamara," he said on a groan, loosening his hold a little, opening his eyes to look down at her.

She gave him a glowing smile.

Carefully rolling to his side, keeping them joined, he pulled her with him. She tucked her head beneath his chin. He felt her lips brush the base of his throat and wanted to lie there forever, just the two of them, holding on tight to each other in the bright morning light.

But forever didn't last all that long. Too soon, the fussy sounds of a hungry baby started in from the monitor on the nightstand.

Jace nuzzled her cheek. "You think maybe he'll go back to sleep?"

She laughed. "Yeah. Good luck with that." The cries on the monitor grew louder, more insistent.

He kissed her. "I'll be right back," he promised as he rolled out of bed and grabbed for his jeans.

Ten minutes later, the baby had stopped crying, but Jace hadn't returned. Tamara pulled on her clothes and headed for the stairs, meeting Jace just as he was starting upward with Frankie cradled in his arms. The baby seemed to be scowling as he sucked hard on his pacifier.

"I changed him," Jace announced with pride when she joined him at the foot of the stairs. "That took a while. This boy knows how to fill a diaper."

She almost laughed. Apparently, Jace was going to be one of those fathers—proud of everything his son did, including the mess he could make in his diaper.

Jace went on, "I rocked him for a bit to settle him down, but I'm thinking he's probably hungry."

As if on cue, Frankie released the pacifier and let out a wail.

Jace slanted her a look. "What do you think?"

She thought he was the hottest, sweetest man in the world, holding that crying baby so tenderly against his broad, muscular bare chest.

"Come on," she said. "Let's warm up his formula and get some coffee going."

"Good idea. Hand me my shirt?"

She grabbed it off the chair and held Frankie while he put it on.

In the kitchen, she made the coffee and he fed the baby. Then they traded places. She held Frankie and he whipped them up some ham and eggs.

He set a plate in front of her. "Here, I'll take him."

Then he sat down with her and ate, holding Frankie with his free arm. Tamara hadn't realized how hungry she was until she took the first bite.

They ate in silence for a while until Jace said, "Let's drive into town. We can take Frankie grocery shopping, and then I need to pick up a few things at the hardware store."

"Seriously?" Tamara pushed her empty plate away and sipped more coffee. "You want to take Frankie shopping?"

"Yep." Jace ate his last bite of scrambled eggs and gazed down at the little guy cradled in his free arm. "Sounds like fun, doesn't it?" he asked the baby.

Tamara reached down to pet Bailey, who'd stretched

out beside her chair. From her other side, Luna let out a hopeful whine. Tamara gave the big Newfoundland a scratch between the ears.

As she petted the dogs, she watched Jace holding Frankie and tried really hard to remember all the reasons she wasn't going to fall hopelessly in love with either the handsome firefighter *or* that beautiful baby, who looked like an angel right now, just lying there quietly in Jace's arms, staring at nothing in particular.

"He's barely three weeks old," she said. "You probably shouldn't go dragging him around town if you don't have to, Jace."

He sent her a reproachful glance. "He'll be fine. And we have a whole day in front of us to do whatever we please."

"Right. And what you want to do is run errands."

"Errands can be fun. We can check out some of the shops on Commercial Street, too. Maybe hit that new cupcake shop. And what kid doesn't like Sadie's Holiday House?" Sadie's shop was a miracle of Christmas treasures year-round. She also offered great gifts and merchandise for all four seasons.

"I think Frankie might be a little young to appreciate the wonders of Sadie's Holiday House—or cupcakes, for that matter."

Someone knocked on the front door.

Tamara put up a hand as Jace moved to stand.

"You've got baby privileges. Stay where you are. I'll get the door."

"Thanks." He gave her that smile, the one that made her heart ache in a really good way.

It was his brother Billy, who gave her a nod as he swept off his hat. "Hey, Tamara. Jace around?"

She led him into the kitchen. "How about some coffee?"

Billy shook his head. "Can't stay." He eyed the baby in Jace's arms. "They're so cute when they're little. Wait till he's sixteen, though. Talk to me then."

Jace asked, "What's going on?"

Billy launched into some story about downed fences and cattle on the loose. "Need your help if you can swing it. Mom says she'll be here in half an hour or so to take over with Frankie."

Jace let out a slow, reluctant sigh. Tamara could feel his frustration. He wanted to spend the day with her and the baby. She wanted that, too. But for more than two weeks he'd been all about Frankie. At some point, he needed to step up and carry his weight on the Bonnie B.

"I'll look after the baby until your mom gets here," Tamara offered.

Jace scowled. "That's not right."

Tamara waved a hand. "You heard Billy. Bonnie will be here in half an hour. Let me help."

"Sorry, you two." Billy twisted the brim of his hat. "I know it's bad timing."

"Hey." Jace gave his brother a dip of his chin. "It's called ranching. It's not like I'm unfamiliar with the working conditions. I'll meet you out at the horse barn."

"'Preciate it." Billy nodded at Tamara. "Good to see you."

"You, too, Billy."

When the door closed behind Jace's brother, Tamara held out her arms. "Give me that little sweetheart."

"I'll just stick around until my mom—"

"Jace, you need to get going. We both know it. Stop stalling."

"Thank you," he said sincerely as he rose and passed her the baby, pausing in the middle of the transfer to brush a kiss across her lips. "I had so many great plans for today," he grumbled when he stepped away.

"No sulking." She glanced down at the baby in her arms. Right now, he wore a blissed-out expression.

Jace asked a bit sheepishly, "I suppose there's no chance I can talk you into staying here and waiting around for me all day?"

There was so much she ought to be doing at home. "Not this time."

"You know, if you did decide to stick around, I swear I'll make it worth your while when I get back."

She lifted the baby to her shoulder and patted his

back. "Are you trying to tempt me with sexual favors?" Frankie burped.

Jace's green eyes twinkled. "Is it working?"

It was—but no way would she admit it. "I really do have a long list of chores to do and errands of my own to run."

He blew out a breath. "I hear you." And then he bent close again and guided a curl of hair behind her ear, his rough finger brushing her skin so lightly, stirring fire in its wake. "You made my day this morning. No, scratch that." His voice was low, sandpaper rough. "You made my year. My decade. My quarter century. My—"

"Stop." She groaned through a laugh. "Get out of here before your big brother decides I'm a bad influence."

He kissed her again, hard and quick this time, pressed his lips to Frankie's fat little cheek and then headed upstairs. Five minutes later, he came down wearing frayed jeans and a faded shirt over a worn tee. After one quick peck, he was out the door.

Bonnie arrived right on time. She bustled into Jace's bedroom, where Tamara sat with Frankie in Jace's comfy leather rocker/recliner.

"You look good with that baby in your arms," Bonnie announced in a whisper. "Is he asleep?"

"Not quite."

"Are you hungry, Tamara? Want some coffee?"

"No. We had breakfast already, and I've had more than my share of coffee for the day."

Bonnie wore a secret smile. "You and Jace seem to be getting along nicely."

She answered sincerely. "He's a great guy, Bonnie."

"Yes, he is." Bonnie glowed with motherly pride. Bending close, she made a cooing sound at Frankie—and then asked in hopeful tone, "You want me to take him?"

She didn't. She could sit here all day, just watching him sleep, waiting for Jace to return and tempt her with those sexual favors he was way too good at. But her fridge at home wouldn't stock itself. "If you would, yes. I need to get going."

"Jace would love it if you stayed." Bonnie always seemed so eager to have Tamara stick around. Should she be pleased about that? Probably. But Bonnie kind of made her nervous. Jace's mom pushed too hard, and Tamara didn't know what to make of her constant matchmaking.

"I really can't." She rose. "Here you go."

With a sigh, Bonnie took the baby.

Jace called that evening at a little past eight.

Just the sound of his voice when he said, "Miss you," made Tamara long for him.

Which was a little over the top, wasn't it? She'd

been with him just that morning, yet here she was, missing him?

Was she getting too attached?

It seemed so. Suddenly, she felt somehow connected to him, giddy at the thought of seeing him, pining for more time with him.

Okay, yeah. She'd kind of felt that way about him before she'd climbed into bed with him—but since this morning, the feeling had intensified times a hundred. Before, she'd been attracted to him, and she'd found herself thinking of him way too often. But now...

Now she yearned to be with him. She wanted to feel his arms around her, to snuggle up close to him, to kiss him and hold him and not let him go.

"You have Friday off?" he asked.

"Yeah. And Saturday."

"That's what I was hoping you'd say. Don't forget. Friday night, you and me. Dinner at The Association."

"I remember."

"Robin will come over to watch Frankie for me that night. I want you to pack an overnight bag."

She was smiling—she couldn't help herself. "Oh, you do, do you?"

"Yes, I do. After dinner, I want to bring you home with me. You can spend the night and then you and me and Frankie can have all day Saturday together."

"Jace, I—"

"Hold your horses. I'm not finished yet." He sounded so pleased with all his plans.

"Sorry. Go on."

"Well, I just wanted to say that I will promise to get you back to your house by eight Saturday night. You'll be fresh, well rested and ready for work Sunday morning."

It all sounded perfect.

Too perfect, and she knew it. Her feelings for him kept getting stronger. Emotionally, she was a runaway train right now, speeding downhill, probably headed for disaster if she couldn't find a way to make herself put on the brakes.

But she didn't *want* to put on the brakes. She wanted to go for it, have her night out with him Friday, go back to the ranch with him afterward and make beautiful love—and then spend all of Saturday hanging around with him and Frankie.

Because, truly, life was short and there were no guarantees. The past was just that. Done and gone. Yes, it had only been a couple of months since she'd walked in on Eric and Elise going at it.

So what? Dr. Eric Pearce was a cheating sleazeball and a big disappointment—and Jace Abernathy was as different from Eric as a man could get.

"Tamara? You still with me?"

"Yes, Jace. I'm right here."

"So what do you think about my weekend plans?"

She hesitated, but only for a second. "I love your plans."

"That's a yes, then?"

"That's a yes."

"To all of it?"

"Yes."

"Yes!" he repeated with a boatload of enthusiasm. "It's my new favorite word to hear from those fine lips of yours—and there's no way I'm waiting till Friday to see you."

A happy thrill shivered through her at the way he kept pushing to see her. She loved that next weekend just wasn't enough for him—she loved it and she needed to get a grip. "Jace, be realistic. I have to work and so do you. And there's Frankie to consider. He's a full-time job in himself."

"Yeah, but I'm going to hire a nanny this week—you just watch me. That'll help. And I was also thinking that maybe Wednesday or Thursday Frankie and I could pick you up at the hospital around noon or so."

"Pick me up for what?"

"For your lunch break. We could go to that cupcake place in Bronco Heights I was telling you about—I mean, it's just for an hour, and I'll get you back to work on time to finish your shift."

"Oh, Jace—"

"I can't wait a whole week. Don't do that to me, Tamara."

She groaned—but she was smiling. "You're really laying it on thick, you know?"

"Yeah. But is it working?"

It was. It really was. "Okay. That new cupcake place, Wednesday. I'll be waiting for you outside the hospital at eleven thirty."

"We'll be there."

"One hour. That's all I've got."

"We will have you back at work on time."

He kept her talking for another twenty minutes. Then Frankie started fussing and he had to go. When she ended the call, she noticed that Harley, tucked up close to her on the bed, was watching her.

"What?" she demanded and scratched him around the ruff of his neck. His tags jingled like bells. "I really like him, Harley," she confessed. "And Frankie is the sweetest little guy in the world. The two of them together—words don't do them justice. That great big man with his gentle ways and that beautiful little baby he'll do anything for…"

Harley yawned hugely.

"You're such a cynic," she accused.

Harley only yawned again.

Jace and Frankie were waiting at the curb in Jace's crew cab when Tamara walked out the hospital's sliding glass door late Wednesday morning.

She felt a giant grin take over her face as Jace jumped out, ran around and opened the passenger door with a flourish. Her soft-soled work shoes couldn't get her to him fast enough.

"I thought Wednesday would never come," he said when she stood beside him.

"I know, right?" she teased. "It's been two whole days." And then she was stepping closer instead of getting into the truck. "Hi," she said, her voice downright breathless, like some long-gone lovestruck fool.

"Hi." And he kissed her.

That kiss might have gone on a little longer than appropriate for the middle of the day at the hospital entrance.

Neither of them seemed to care—she certainly didn't.

When she finally dropped back to her heels, he said, "Let's go."

She climbed up into the seat and he shut the door. Turning, she tried to get a look at Frankie. The car seat was buckled in facing the rear of the vehicle for safety, so all she saw was the top of his head drooping toward the window.

Jace climbed into the driver's seat and pulled his door closed firmly.

"Shh," she whispered. "He's asleep."

Jace shrugged. "He's fine. He's probably going to wake up when we get there, anyway. Buckle up." He leaned across the console and kissed her again.

She smiled against his warm lips and reached for her seat belt.

* * *

A narrow brick building wedged between an antique shop and a beauty salon, Kendra's Cupcakes had a big front display window framed in a rim of brick. The name of the shop, in flowing red letters, spanned the front window. A small awning of red and white stripes shaded the glass front door. A bell overhead tinkled merrily when Jace pulled the door open.

Tamara pushed Frankie's stroller over the threshold.

Inside, it smelled like heaven. Glass display cases showed off the most gorgeous cupcakes she'd ever seen, along with mouthwatering pies, cookies and cakes.

A pretty blonde woman called out a greeting. "Welcome!"

Tamara briefly conferred with Jace. Then she took Frankie to one of the little round café tables on one side of the store, and he went to place their order.

The shop was pretty busy. There was a line at the counter, and as she waited for Jace, two women in their fifties or thereabouts took the one remaining empty table.

"What a beautiful little baby!" said one of the women. "I'm guessing by the blue hat that it's a boy."

"How old is he?" demanded the other lady.

"Three weeks," Tamara provided.

"He looks so sweet and peaceful."

The first woman chuckled. "Don't they all look like angels when they're sleeping?"

About then, the other woman spotted Jace as he stepped up to the counter to place their order. "Oh! Renée, isn't that our famous firefighter?" The woman blinked and looked down at Frankie again. "And, oh, my! I'll bet that this little angel is baby Frankie, am I right?"

"Yes, this is Frankie."

"Oh, he is adorable. Look at that little face." The woman's sharp gaze strayed toward the counter again. "And that man…" She plunked her hand against her chest. "Well, what can I say? It does my heart good when things work out as they should. I'm sure he's a splendid father."

"Yes. Yes, he is."

"Doris, dear." The first woman patted her friend's hand. "Let's just leave our packages here and go on up to order together."

Doris agreed. The two rose and headed for the counter as Jace, with a tray of goodies and two coffees, turned for their table.

Doris and Renée converged on him. One patted his arm and the other clasped his shoulder. He nodded and chatted with them quietly for a moment, and then they moved on toward the counter.

"It's so hard being famous," Tamara teased in a whisper when he set the tray down on their table.

"Can't complain. I'm grateful for people like

Doris and Renée. They're the reason I'm Frankie's foster dad right now. You sure all you want is this giant maple bacon cupcake?"

"It's giant, all right." It was the size of Jace's fist.

"You should eat some protein first," he chided. "After all, you've got more than half your shift ahead of you."

"I had a good, healthy breakfast. And a nurse does not live on protein alone." She peeled back the bright cupcake liner and nibbled off a bite. A shameless groan escaped her. "So good. I might be in heaven— and you are my hero for bringing me here."

The smile he gave her was slow and full of intimate promises. "So I'm thinking that when I finally get you all to myself again, you'll be showing me lots of gratitude."

She groaned again as she swallowed another perfect, bacon-y, maple-y bite, and Jace gave a low, suggestive chuckle. Sometimes he seemed like the most innocent man she'd ever known—good to the core with a heart as open as the wide Montana sky.

That chuckle, though? That look in his eye? Smoking hot and dangerous, too.

A beautiful little girl with wavy blond hair and a giant smile greeted the young couple two tables over and gave them each an extra red-and-white-striped napkin.

A moment later, the little cutie was beaming up at Tamara. "Hi. I'm Mila." She pointed a thumb at the name tag pinned to her ruffled red-and-white apron. "Are you a nurse?"

"Yes, I am."

"I thought so because you're wearing what nurses wear."

"They're called scrubs."

"Why?"

"It's short for 'scrubbing in,' which is something we do when we're going to help out with—" *Surgery* seemed a little too technical for Mila, so she settled on, "an operation."

Mila nodded as though she understood. "Do all nurses wear scrubs?"

"Sometimes we don't—and many other hospital workers wear scrubs. Not just nurses."

Tamara's explanation was apparently way more than enough for the little girl because she suddenly asked brightly, "Do you want some more napkins?" She went right ahead and answered her own question. "Here you go—two for you." She handed a couple to Tamara, then turned and plunked down two more by Jace's plate. "And two for you. Is that enough?"

Tamara smiled. "Perfect."

"When you eat my mom's cupcakes, you really need lots of napkins."

"Thank you." Tamara used one to dab at the bit of frosting in the corner of her mouth.

"That's my mommy," the little girl announced

with pride as she waved at the pretty blonde woman behind the counter.

Jace asked, "How long have you worked here, Mila?"

"Oh, I don't work. I'm seven. I'm just helping my mommy."

"That's nice of you."

"I like to help."

In the stroller, Frankie let out a small cry. Tamara took the stroller handle and gently rolled it back and forth. Frankie sighed.

Mila set her stack of napkins on the table and crossed around behind Tamara's chair to get a closer look at the baby. "So cute. I like babies."

"Me, too," said Jace with a wink for Tamara.

Mila replied earnestly, "He's a boy, isn't he?"

"How did you guess?" Jace asked.

"Mommies usually dress baby girls up in pink with ribbons and bows and stuff. What's his name?"

"Frankie."

"His hat is so cute. It has bear ears!" Mila looked up at Jace with a dreamy expression. "It's so nice... A daddy, a mommy and a little baby boy."

Tamara considered correcting her, maybe explaining that she and Jace were—what? Just friends? After what they'd shared Monday morning, *just friends* wouldn't cover it. Not by a long shot. And, anyway, what did it matter? Whatever she might say just seemed like way more information than an adorable seven-year-old could possibly want or need.

Mila flashed a brave smile at Jace. "I don't have a daddy. My mommy and me are a whole family all by ourself, but sometimes I think that a daddy would be—"

"Mila!" the blonde woman called gently from behind the counter. "Please let our visitors enjoy their treats."

"Okay, Mommy!" Mila scooted back around the table and grabbed her stack of napkins. "I better get busy. Everybody needs more napkins." And off she went.

As soon as Mila was a few tables away, her mom approached with a coffee pot and refilled their cups. "I'm sorry. My daughter loves interacting with everyone, but she forgets that people need time to eat their cupcakes." She laughed. "I'm Kendra Humphrey, by the way. Hope you folks will visit us again soon."

"Definitely," Tamara replied. "I had the maple bacon cupcake. It was so good, I'm white-knuckling it to keep from having a second one."

Kendra chuckled. "Wait till you try my Death-by-Chocolate Cake."

Tamara groaned. "Now, you're just being cruel."

"Next time, maybe," Kendra suggested.

"We'll be back." Jace was nodding. "No question about that."

Kendra Humphrey moved on with a bright smile. A moment later, she caught up with her daughter and ushered the little girl back behind the counter.

Thinking of her own long-gone father, of all the years wishing and hoping that he might show a little interest in her someday, Tamara watched the sweet little girl go.

"Hey." The man across the table laid his big, rough hand over hers. "Why the sad face all of a sudden?" He kept his voice low, just between them.

"That little girl really wants a dad."

"She's a sweetheart. And that's got a lot to do with her mom."

"And your point is…?"

"They look like a winning team to me—Mila and her mom. I'm guessing that any day now some smart, single cowboy is going to walk in that glass door and realize that he can't wait to be Mila's dad."

"You're such a complete romantic."

Now he was grinning. "Admit it. You love that about me."

She couldn't deny it—because he was right.

"It was fun," she said, when he pulled to a stop in front of the hospital's main entrance. "Thanks for taking me to Kendra's Cupcakes." She felt for the door latch.

He took her other hand. "Wait a minute." His fingers curled around hers. "Tonight…"

A flash of heat raced over her skin. She tried to be practical. "Jace, you've got Frankie to think about." She spoke quietly in order not to disturb the baby snoozing in the back seat. "And I have to work tomorrow early. So do you for that matter, right?"

He brought her hand to his lips. His breath was so warm drifting over her skin. "I don't care. I need to see you. I need to hold you."

"It's only two nights. We'll see each other Friday for dinner, and I'll come out to the ranch with you afterward."

"And tonight, I'll come to your house."

"You're not listening."

"I won't keep you up late. Just for a little while, an hour or two."

She shook her head, but her traitorous heart was shouting *yes*! "Think about Frankie. You can't go dragging him all the way to Bronco Valley just for—"

"—a little time alone with you? Yes, I can." He gave a gentle tug on her hand, and she didn't even pretend to resist as she leaned across the console again. "Tamara..."

"Oh, Jace..."

And then he was kissing her. His lips felt like heaven and her breath came too fast. It took every ounce of will she possessed to pull back to her side of the truck.

"We'll be at your house at seven thirty, Frankie and me."

"No."

His full lips formed a thin line—but he didn't argue. That was another thing she loved about him. He was all man and he made his desires known, but when she gave him a flat no, he stopped pushing.

And suddenly, she couldn't bear the weight of both his disappointment *and* hers. "Fine," she said. "Okay. Tonight, then."

His face lit up. "Yeah?"

She nodded. "But I'll come out to the ranch."

"No, Tamara. That's not right."

"Yes, it is."

"I'm the one pushing for time with you tonight. The least I can do is come to you."

"Uh-uh. It's better for Frankie if I come to you. That way he can be nice and cozy in his own bassinet. I will stay until ten. Absolutely no later."

Jace eased his big hand around the nape of her neck and pulled her close. Their lips met again.

Kissing Jace? Nothing compared.

"I'm selfish," he whispered against her parted lips. "But I still want to see you tonight too much to let you off the hook."

And she confessed, "I want to see you, too. Now, let me go before HR writes me up for inappropriate behavior in plain view of the reception desk."

"They wouldn't really do that, would they?"

She leaned his way once more, just long enough for a last quick, hard kiss. "I don't know. But let's not tempt fate."

That time when she reached for the door latch, he didn't try to stop her.

And that evening, he was waiting on the porch, the door wide open behind him, when she pulled her RAV4 to a stop in front of his cabin.

"Frankie?" she asked as she ran up the front steps.

He waved the silent baby monitor. "Out like a light."

She threw herself at him, twining her arms around his neck, lifting her lips to his.

He plundered her mouth. Nothing had ever felt so right as his kiss. Circling her waist with one powerful arm, he lifted her.

She took that as a signal and wrapped her legs good and tight around his lean hips. Oh, she could feel him, straining the zipper of his jeans.

Turning, he carried her through the open door, kicking it shut behind him.

Upstairs, he paused only to set the monitor on the nightstand. And then, kissing her madly as she kissed him right back, he began to undress her.

She got right to work on the buttons of his shirt. In no time, everything they'd been wearing was strewn across the rug by the bed.

He scooped her up again and kissed her some more—long, sweet, perfect kisses. "So beautiful," he whispered, lifting her and setting her on the bed. "It's been too long since I had you here in my bed."

That made her laugh, a low, throaty sound she hardly recognized as her own. "Two whole days," she teased him. "How did we survive?"

"Barely," he growled low.

That made her laugh again—the sound even huskier than before. There was something about him. He made her feel like the sexiest, prettiest, most irresistible woman alive. Now they were alone together, all her inhibitions drifted right out the window and floated away into the wide, starry night sky.

He scraped his teeth down the side of her throat, slowly, lightly. She shuddered in arousal as he pressed a line of hot kisses across her collarbone, pausing at the vulnerable notch in the middle to dip his tongue in.

She moaned. It felt so good, his tongue on her flesh, wet and sweet and eager.

But then that mouth of his was on the move again, his lips trailing back up the side of her neck. He caught her earlobe between his teeth. She sighed as he whispered, "I'm trying not to rush you, not to take this too fast." She assumed he was talking about tonight, about the two of them, naked in the upstairs bed. But then he added, "I can't help what I feel, though. I want you here, with me, Tamara. I want you here all the time."

She caught his face between her hands. "Look at me."

He met her gaze. "I never want to look anywhere else."

"It's too soon for that kind of talk, Jace."

"I know."

"Then why say it?"

"Because you're here with me and I'm holding you and the truth just… Well, sometimes the truth is bound to slip out."

She dropped her hands to her sides and turned her head away. Because she wanted to believe him way too much.

"Come on," he coaxed. "Look at me." She made herself do it and he said, "You're afraid."

"I didn't say that." *But I am.* "I said it's too soon."

"Yeah. I know. I hear you."

"Don't ever lie to me, Jace."

"Never."

"Or cheat on me."

"I wouldn't. No way. Because cheating is wrong. Even if you weren't you, I wouldn't do that."

"What do you mean, if I weren't me?"

"I mean that I am not a cheater under any circumstances. I also mean that *because* you're you, I would never want to cheat, anyway."

"Oh, please."

He narrowed his eyes at her. "Don't do that. Don't act hard. You're not. You just put on that hardness to try to protect yourself. Because at the center of you, you're soft and giving. You're all goodness, Tamara. You care. You care a lot and you show it every day. It's why you're a nurse, because taking care of people, helping them—that's second nature to you."

She hardly knew what to say to all that, so she challenged, "And what about you?"

"Me? I do what I can for others, too."

"Yeah. You do."

"And I'm an Abernathy to the core."

"Which means…?"

"An Abernathy is truehearted. Yeah, sometimes it takes us a while to find the right one, the one we're meant to be with, but once we finally do, we never stray."

Looking in his eyes now, she absolutely believed him. She knew that *he* believed in doing the right thing. In helping other people. In the kind of love that lasted a lifetime.

And why wouldn't he believe in forever? His mother and father were still together, still going strong after decades of marriage. He'd lived on this ranch his whole life, surrounded by family, secure in who he was, satisfied with his place in the world.

He hadn't grown up the way she had, with a self-absorbed mother, an absent father and a series of stepfathers who considered her no more than someone they would have to put up with, an obligation they'd taken on when they'd married her mother.

"Tamara…" He kissed her name onto her lips. She opened for him, pulling him closer.

He kissed her some more, stroked those big hands over her skin, touching her so ardently she couldn't help but surrender.

"Tamara…" He whispered her name again, his voice rough, reverent, tender.

And those doubts of hers, they scattered and fled, gone as though they'd never been.

Yeah, they would be back, her doubts. Love had not been kind to her. She would need time to learn to trust him unconditionally. If in fact she ever could.

Trust just didn't come easy. Not for a lot of people—and especially not for her.

Chapter Nine

"It's after ten, Jace." They stood by the driver's door of her SUV. "I really have to go." She went on tiptoe to kiss him.

He couldn't resist gathering her in, cradling her closer and taking the kiss deeper. She melted in his arms, a good sign.

Reluctantly, he let her go—but caught hold of her hand before she could turn and pull open the driver's door.

"What?" she demanded, adorably suspicious.

Okay, maybe he shouldn't do what he was going to do next. He'd pushed her hard enough already tonight, trying to chip away at those tall, thick walls around her heart.

But he needed to find ways to show her that she

could give him her trust. So he pried her fingers open and set the spare key in the heart of her palm. "In case you need to let yourself in sometime."

"Jace." She huffed out a breath, trying so hard to be tough. "This isn't necessary."

He shrugged. "Take it anyway. Just in case." He folded her fingers around it.

Clearly trying to hide a pleased smile, she scoffed, "You're impossible."

"You're beautiful." He dropped a kiss right between her big brown eyes. And then he opened her door for her. She got in. "Drive safe. I'll call you tomorrow night. Just to check in, you know. See how you're doing."

Those brown eyes were soft, completely open to him—at least for the moment. "Good night, Jace."

"Night, beautiful."

Back inside, he heard fussy sounds coming from his bedroom. The fussing turned to crying.

Jace warmed a bottle. He sat in the rocker/recliner to feed the little guy. As Frankie sucked happily away, Jace felt great about everything. He and Frankie were a team already.

And every moment he spent with Tamara had him feeling more certain that she was the one for him, that the three of them should be together.

He grinned, thinking of that, of him and Tamara and Frankie making a family. Most people would probably say he was moving too fast, that just adjusting to having Frankie ought to be enough for him.

And maybe those people were right.

Too bad. A man didn't get what he wanted by telling himself that what he already had was enough.

Tamara was feeling great when she left the hospital Thursday evening. Three babies had been born that day, each one healthy, each birth free of complications. She'd had lunch with Stephanie and they'd talked about going out together with the guys some time in the next few weeks.

The guys…

Yep. That was how they spoke of Jace and Geoff now. *The guys.*

Meaning *their* guys.

And even though it scared her a little, Tamara did think of Jace that way already. As *her* guy.

Yeah, okay, maybe this thing with him was happening way too fast.

But it just seemed so right with him. Once or twice the past couple of days, she'd actually let herself think the *L* word. Still, she tried hard to keep a rein on her emotions, tried to go slow, not to get too wrapped up in him too swiftly.

Going slow wasn't really working, though. He was so open, so sincere. So *real* with her. He had no trouble just putting it right out there—that she already meant a lot to him, that he wanted to be with her every chance he got. She kept trying to resist him, to keep both feet firmly on the ground. But Jace...

He made her feel like she was floating on clouds. When she tried to be tough, he coaxed her to soften, every time.

With him, her heart already felt all in.

At home, she cuddled Harley for a few minutes and then whipped up a chef's salad for dinner. Jace called at eight thirty. They talked for an hour, laughing together, teasing each other.

And he had news. "I hired a nanny. Her name is Sonia. Her kids are grown, and she and her husband, Rob, have ten acres bordering the Bonnie B."

"So she won't be living in?"

"Nope. But she wants full-time, forty hours a week, give or take, and she says she can work a flexible schedule. She was looking after twin girls in town, but the mother decided to stay home with them."

"You like her."

"I do. She and my mom are friends. I've known her forever. Sonia is calm and capable and easy to be around. She'll be over tomorrow at four thirty in the morning."

"An early riser."

"She knows ranch work, so she expects to be starting her day well before dawn. Robin will watch Frankie tomorrow night so I can take you to The Association. Pick you up at six?"

"I'll be ready."

When she hung up, she had a long, lazy bath and then settled into bed with Harley purring at her side and a yummy romance on her e-reader. She was enjoying just one more chapter, looking forward to sleeping in tomorrow, when her mom called.

Olivia opened the conversation with a long sigh. "Well, Nigel's off to Vegas again. I'm here on my own."

"Mom, you ought to go with him."

"He's working. It's just business, business, business. If I'm going to be lonely, I might as well be in my own house—which reminds me, there's someone I want you to meet."

"Mom, I'm really not interested in—"

"Oh, you will love him. He is the sweetest man. Forty-five, recently divorced. Two children. But really, the ex-wife is the primary caregiver, so it's not ever going to be a problem if for some reason you and the kiddies don't hit it off."

"Mom, honestly, I—"

"I know, I know. You *love* children and I'm sure you will make an amazing stepmom. I was just letting you know up front that it's not as if you've got to stay at home full-time and look after them. His name is David. David Nicholas. He's a neurosurgeon. Lives here, right on the golf course. We met him at the club. He and Nigel are involved in a couple of projects together."

Where to even start with this?

In a patient, level voice, she said, "Mom, I'm not interested. In fact, I'm seeing someone here in Bronco." Tamara closed her eyes. She shouldn't have said that. It was way too early to tell her mother about Jace.

"Did you just say you're seeing someone new?" her mother demanded.

Tamara gritted her teeth. "Yes, I did."

"But, honey, you only broke up with the doctor a few weeks ago." Tamara's mom greatly admired what she called "professional" men. Eric Pearce had qualified as a professional because he had MD after his name. While Tamara was dating him, Olivia had eased off the constant refrain that Tamara should quit her job, sell her house and leave Bronco behind.

"It's been more than two months since I broke up with Eric, Mom. And correct me if I'm mistaken, but haven't you just been trying to set me up with this David guy?"

"That's different."

Don't ask, she warned herself. And then she did. "Different, how?"

"Well, darling, I *know* David."

"And I know Jace."

"Jace. Hmm. I'm sure you *think* you know him."

Beside her, Harley purred louder than usual and stretched out a sleek paw to rest it on her thigh. He'd always been that way, picking up her darker moods, trying to soothe her. Right now, he gazed up at her through low-lidded eyes, as if to say, *Love you, human. Chill.*

Her mother said, too sweetly, "Tell me about Jace... Does he have a last name?"

"Yeah, Mom. Abernathy. Jace Abernathy. He's a wonderful guy—a rancher and a volunteer firefighter who has just become a foster dad to an orphaned newborn boy."

"He's a *foster* parent?" her mother repeated in a disbelieving tone. Apparently, the ranching and firefighting were hard enough for her to wrap her mind around.

"Yes. He's hoping to adopt the baby, but that's a whole other process and will take a while."

"Well. Ranching, firefighting and being a foster dad. It sounds like Jace Abernathy has his hands full. I suppose you're helping him out any way you can." It was a dig, delivered with a coating of saccharine sweetness.

Tamara answered with pride. "Yes, I am."

"Oh, darling." Suddenly, Olivia sounded infinitely weary. "You have such a kind heart."

"Mom, having a kind heart is a *good* thing."

"Of course it is."

"Then why do you make it sound like a criticism?"

"But I'm not!"

"Look. Let's not argue."

"I assure you, sweetheart, the last thing I called to do is to argue with you."

"Good," Tamara replied with forced cheerfulness. Because there was no point in losing her temper. Blowing her top never worked with her mom. During her teen years and early twenties, she used to get into it with Olivia all the time, calling her out for her snobbery and her priorities that were not in any way Tamara's priorities.

But getting into it with her mom never did either of them any good. Her mom never changed—and neither did Tamara, for that matter. Nowadays, Tamara made it a point to be honest with Olivia. She tried really hard not to judge her mom or to lose her temper when they talked. Getting angry only led to her saying things she would later regret.

"So, anyway," Tamara went on, "I'm seeing Jace Abernathy. I really like him. And as I explained the last time we talked, I can't come to visit you until the holidays at the earliest."

"Just tell me, darling. Be honest. Is this Jace Abernathy person self-supporting?"

"As a matter of fact, he is. Very much so."

"Well. I'm relieved to hear it."

Tamara stifled a groan. "Mom, this conversation is going nowhere fast. It's time for us to say good night."

Her mother made a small, thoughtful sound. "Hmm. Well, if he's not a deadbeat, it's probably about the baby, then…" She let her voice trail off, leaving room for Tamara to ask what she meant. Tamara didn't ask. She already knew. Olivia continued on without prompting. "Darling. Think about it. You said he wants permanent custody, and that would be a much smoother process, I'm sure, if he were married to someone like you. Someone who's obviously going to be a good wife and a fine mother to that orphaned child."

Olivia's cynical take on Jace's motive for pursuing her hit Tamara where it hurt. She'd never even considered that Jace might be seeing her as a way to help him get permanent custody of Frankie.

No. Uh-uh. Jace just didn't think like that. He really did care for her. She saw it in his eyes every time he looked at her. She felt it in his touch.

But then again, he was also deeply committed to adopting and raising Frankie…

"Tamara? Are you still there?"

She debated what to do. Just hang up? Tell her mother she was full of crap? "I'm here."

"Oh. I know that tone. Now you're angry with me, aren't you? Well, I'm sorry. But I call it as I see it."

"I don't think you're the least bit sorry, Mom."

"Now I get attitude?"

"Yeah, I think you deserve a little attitude about now. You do not know Jace. You've never met him. And yet you're willing to say insulting things about him in order to try to hook me up with some guy you met at your country club."

"I never—"

"Mom. I'm hanging up now. Please don't call me again until you're honestly ready to say that you're sorry for the way you've behaved on this call. I love you, and I'll talk to you later. Good night." She ended the call.

Tossing the phone on the nightstand, she glared at the far wall and let out a low, growling sound that caused Harley to jump from the bed and head for the door. "Sorry, baby!" she called after the cat.

Harley didn't answer. He just kept walking, his skinny black tail held high.

Punching her pillow, she flopped to her back. For a while, she stared up at the ceiling and thought of all the things she should have said to her mom.

Slowly her heart rate returned to normal. She reminded herself that her mom was not and never had been a happy woman. Tamara couldn't make Olivia happy. Only Olivia could do that.

Best case scenario, in a few days her mom would call back and apologize. If that didn't happen, Tamara would eventually get in touch again and work it out with her.

No, they didn't have the greatest relationship. But at least Olivia had always been there. Unlike Tamara's father, her mom had never walked away. Being there counted.

It counted for a lot.

As for the possibility that Jace wanted her chiefly as a potential mother to Frankie, one who would look good on paper for Child and Family Services, well, she couldn't believe that. It really wasn't like Jace at all.

"Wow." Jace swept off his hat when Tamara answered the door that night. She wore a silky midnight blue dress, and her high-heeled black shoes made her fine legs look even more beautiful than usual. Her thick brown hair, loose on her bare shoulders, gleamed with hints of bronze under the porch light.

She grinned and looked down at her dress. "What? This ol' thing?"

He took off his hat. "You really do take my breath away."

Her soft cheeks had turned the sweetest shade of pink. "Well, then. Mission accomplished."

"Overnight bag?" he reminded her, hoping she hadn't changed her mind about staying the night with him at the ranch.

His smile got wider when she answered, "Right here," and scooped up a bag from the table on her side of the door. He took it and hooked it on his shoulder.

Her cat chose that moment to slip out the door.

"No, you don't." Jace plunked his hat back on his head, dipped to a crouch, scooped Harley close and scratched him under the chin. "Purring like a brand-new John Deere tractor. I think he *wanted* me to catch him."

"It's entirely possible. He loves attention. Here, let me have him." Jace passed her the cat as she stepped over the threshold. "You be good now," she said to Harley. "I left you plenty of water and food, and I'll see you tomorrow afternoon." She kissed the cat between his pointy black ears and set him inside. Then she pulled the door shut and locked it.

Jace offered his arm. They went down her front walk to his crew cab, which gleamed in the light from the streetlamp above. He'd had one of the hands drive it to the detail shop he liked in Bronco Heights, so it would be looking good for tonight.

At The Association, he left his truck with the valet and led Tamara into the clubhouse with its high, beamed ceilings, etched glass windows and lamps with art glass shades. The host greeted him by name and led them through a series of lounges furnished in leather and dark wood. Every room had a large fieldstone fireplace. Massive iron chandeliers hung from the giant beams overhead.

"Here we are," said the host at last, stopping at a table tucked away in its own cozy nook. He pulled out an ornate chair with a carved back for Tamara. Once they were settled, he handed them menus and offered a wine list.

When he finally left them alone, Tamara scooted

her chair closer to him and then rearranged her place setting, too. He watched her, thinking that he would never get tired of looking at her.

"I like to be closer," she whispered, leaning his way enough that her shoulder brushed his arm. A hint of her fresh, tempting scent teased him.

"Works for me. The closer, the better."

She glanced up at the art glass fixture overhead. "This place reminds me of an old Western movie," she said. "This would be the scene where all the rich cattlemen drink expensive whiskey and plot how to steal the poor townsfolk's land."

He leaned close and smoothed a sleek swatch of hair behind her ear. "Nothing like that would ever happen in Bronco."

A low laugh escaped her. "I'm so relieved to hear that—and I know all about this place. Not a lot of the members live in Bronco Valley, now, do they?"

He wasn't sure what she was getting at. "You would rather we had dinner somewhere else?"

"What? No! I just…" She seemed to have no idea how to go on.

Curious, he prompted, "You just what?"

She folded her hands in her lap and looked down at them. "I'm being rude. I'm sorry."

"I didn't say that."

"Which is kind of you—but still. You've taken me out for a beautiful dinner. You don't deserve to be treated to my snarky side."

"Hey…" He dared to ease his arm around the back of her chair. Settling his hand lightly on her silky shoulder, he pulled her closer. With a sigh, she leaned into him.

The wine steward came.

Jace loved that Tamara didn't move away. She left her head on his shoulder as he ordered them a nice bottle of red.

Only when they were alone again did she retreat to her own chair. He let her go with reluctance.

Their wine came, along with crusty bread. They ordered wedge salads, filet mignon and baked potatoes slathered in butter, sour cream, bacon and chives.

He kept the talk light until the main dish was served and the wait staff had left them alone.

Then he said, "So…"

She slanted him a resigned glance. "Go ahead. Ask me."

"What stirred up your snarky side?"

She ate a bite of her steak, taking her time about it before grimly answering his question. "My mother. She called last night. She wants me to visit her soon, and I can't get away until the holidays."

"So you feel guilty?"

"I feel frustrated. What she really wants is for me to move back to California, to live near her."

"Are you considering it?" he asked, though he feared he might not like her answer.

Her full lips tightened. "Uh-uh. No way."

Yes! With a mental fist pump, he raised his glass to her. "I'll drink to that."

Tamara smiled at Jace and thought what a great guy he really was.

She picked up her wine and held it up for a toast. "To Bronco."

As they sipped, she considered how much to tell him. He really didn't need to hear how her mom had assumed he must be a deadbeat—or the kind of guy who would use her to get permanent custody of Frankie.

When she set her glass back down, she said, "My mom is difficult. My stepdad is frequently gone on business. She's lonely, which is why she's always after me to come out to California. She and I kind of got into it last night on the phone, and now I'm feeling a little angry at her. When we walked in here, I instantly thought of her."

"She's a member of a cattlemen's club?"

"No, but she would definitely be impressed with this place. She lives on a golf course in a gated community and spends a lot of time at her country club."

"So, what you're telling me is that when she finally comes to visit you, we should bring her here, right?" He wasn't smiling, exactly. But she could see the light of humor in his eyes.

She laughed then. It felt good. "My mother would love to have dinner here."

"Well, okay, then. That's what we'll do."

"Jace, I…"

"What? Say it."

"We don't always get along, my mom and me. But I love her and I know she really does love me. When I was growing up, there were times when it was just Mom and me against the world. Too bad she's never fully accepted that she needs to respect my boundaries. I'm constantly having to remind her to back off. That's never fun. And I really am sorry I took my frustrations with her out on you."

He caught her hand and wove their fingers together. "No need to apologize. I can handle a little snark—and I think I understand how you feel. My mother's a rock. But now and then she gets on my last nerve."

"What?" She faked a look of shock. "You mean my mom's not the only one who forgets to stay on her side of the fence?"

"Not by a long shot." He kissed her, a quick brush of his lips against her cheek as he let go of her hand. "I like that you were honest with me," he whispered in her ear. "That you told me what was bothering you."

Okay, fine. She felt marginally guilty that she hadn't told him all of her mother's crappy remarks. But he didn't need to hear the mean things her mother had said about him. "Well, talking about my mother is not exactly romantic dinner conversation."

"To me it is. I want to know everything about you, Tamara. And your mom is part of that."

"You can't solve my problems for me."

"Believe me, I know—and that's another thing I like about you. You're not asking me to solve your problems. But you *are* letting me know what's going on with you."

His words warmed her. "Enough about my issues with my mother." She picked up her glass again and raised it to him. "I just want to enjoy a beautiful night out with you."

When Tamara and Jace arrived at the cabin, his sister was curled up on the leather sofa in the main room with Luna on one side and Bailey on the other.

The dogs jumped right down and came to Jace. He knelt to give them a little attention, and then they moved on to Tamara, who greeted them with more rubs and pats.

Robin turned off the TV and came toward them.

Jace set Tamara's overnight bag on the coffee table. "Thanks, sis." He pulled Robin into a hug.

"Any time." She grinned up at him. Watching them made Tamara wish she had siblings, people she'd grown up with, people who knew way too much about her and loved her no matter what. "Frankie was adorable," Robin said. "He ate, he burped, he pooped. I changed his diaper. He cried a little. I rocked him and he went back to sleep—all in all, a thrilling evening here at the ranch."

Jace walked her to the door and locked up behind her. When he turned back to Tamara, the look in his eyes caused a warm shiver of yearning to melt her midsection and make her knees go weak.

"You need anything?" His voice was a low, hot rumble.

She drew in a slow, shaky breath. "Just you."

Chapter Ten

Upstairs, Jace put the baby monitor on the night-stand and commanded his two big, sweet dogs to lie down. The dogs sprawled on the rug near the door, and Jace turned to Tamara.

He began to undress her by guiding the satin straps of her dress down her arms. Taking her shoulders, he turned her around.

"So beautiful," he whispered. His warm lips brushed her shoulder as he took her zipper down in a long, lazy glide.

The dress pooled at her feet. She stepped out of it. He scooped it up and set it on the bedside chair.

She perched on the edge of the bed to take off her high-heeled shoes.

"Leave them on," he said in a low voice, as he

shrugged out of his jacket and began unbuttoning his shirt. "For now."

As she sat there watching him, he dropped the shirt and jacket on the chair, toed off his boots and stepped out of his black dress pants and the boxer briefs under them.

Without a stitch on, he held out his hand. A grin lifted one side of his mouth.

She laid her hand in his, and he pulled her to her feet. Again, he guided her to turn around. Dazed in the most thrilling way, she drew a shaky breath at the feel of his big fingers working the hooks at the back of her strapless bra.

He tossed the bra to the chair.

His warm hands clasped her shoulders, and he pulled her against his broad, hard, bare chest. Heat radiated from him. "Tamara…"

She tipped her head back to him. Those wonderful hands of his strayed as he kissed her. His fingers glided over her shoulders and downward until he cupped her breasts, one in either big palm.

A sound escaped her, a groan all tangled up with a sigh. He kissed that sigh off her lips as he caressed her, until her breasts ached in the sweetest way and her nipples were hard little points pressing into his wide palms.

From there, he moved on, stroking down her belly and lower.

She cried out when he parted her. Soon, those fingers had her crooning his name and begging him, "More…"

"This way." He breathed the word against her cheek as he turned her to face him.

"Hmm?" She gazed up at him through heavy-lidded eyes.

He whispered her name once and then again as he dropped a row of kisses down the side of her throat—and lower.

She blinked and looked down to find him on his knees before her.

Framing his face between her hands, she bent and took his mouth. They kissed for the longest time, him below her, still on his knees, her body bent over him, wanting to get closer, wanting to feel him surrounding her, holding her so tight.

But then he took her shoulders and guided her to stand tall. He grasped her waist in either hand as he pressed his lips to the vulnerable flesh below her navel.

Those hands strayed lower. He urged her to part her legs. She took hold of his muscled shoulders to keep from melting into a puddle of longing right there on the bedside rug. With her high-heeled shoes planted wide, she threw her head back and cried out her pleasure to the ceiling.

When she came back to herself, he scooped her up and set her on the bed. "I do like these sexy shoes," he whispered, as he slid one off and then the other.

He joined her on the bed, pulling her close so she could feel him, hot and ready, pressed against her. She heard a husky, sensual laugh and realized it was her own.

And then she was reaching for the bedside drawer, dipping her hand in, getting what they needed. She eased it down over him. "I want you," she whispered as he rose up over her, urging her to part for him.

She wrapped her arms and legs around him, and he came into her in one forceful stroke.

It felt so good, so right, to be joined with him, filled with him, as close as a woman can be to a man. With him, making love was like nothing she'd ever known before. She felt they were connected on a deeper level. Like they were meant to be.

She admired him and she loved being with him.

It was getting really difficult not to let her heart take control.

He rolled to his back and she sat up, folding her legs on either side of him. Riding him, looking down into those steady eyes of his, she wished the moment would never end.

"I want this to go on forever," he said.

She wondered if he'd somehow read her mind. "Oh, me, too."

A dark chuckle escaped him. "But I'm not gonna last too much longer." His big hands clasped her hips, rocking her, following the rhythm her body was setting.

She whispered, "I'm close." Tossing her head,

feeling her hair brushing wildly over her shoulders, down her back, she rolled against him, pressing down, bringing a groan from him.

"Now, Tamara," he commanded roughly.

She let out a cry as she went over the edge. Tumbling into fulfillment, she babbled out a chain of exclamations. "Yes!" and "Please!" and "Just like this, always. Just like this!"

And then he was taking over, surging up into her, finding his own climax in the afterglow of hers.

At midnight, they got up. He pulled on his wrinkled dress pants. She'd left her bag downstairs, so he gave her a soft black T-shirt to wear.

Downstairs, they raided the cupboards.

She grabbed a big box of cereal. "Cinnamon Toast Crunch!" she cried in delight. "You must've known I was coming."

He grinned at that.

She shook a finger at him. "No jokes about coming. I absolutely forbid it."

"Yes, ma'am. Whatever you say."

They were halfway through their bowls of yummy, sugary cereal when Frankie woke up.

"Let me get him." She set down her spoon.

He clasped her arm and pulled her toward him to kiss her quick and sweet. "Of course," he said, his lips on hers.

In Jace's room, Frankie was working up a pretty good head of steam. She checked his diaper. It was wet, so she gave him his pacifier to calm him and then cleaned him up.

As she was lifting him to her shoulder from the changing table, Jace appeared with a bottle. He handed it over and left the room.

She sat in the rocker/recliner and fed Frankie with Bailey snoozing at her feet, thinking how absolutely right it felt to be here holding this sweet boy in her arms in the middle of the night, with Bailey for company.

Again, she reminded herself not to get all swept up in the moment, not to start imagining forever, picturing them all together—Tamara and Jace and Frankie. And Bailey and Luna and Harley, too.

That would be fun, though. Introducing Harley to Jace's dogs. She had a feeling it would go pretty well. His dogs were chill. Harley was the same.

But you never knew for sure with dogs and cats.

She heard a tap.

Jace stood framed in the open doorway, knocking softly on the doorframe. "How's he doing?"

She set the empty bottle on the little table by her chair. "He's fading fast." Rising, she put the baby in the bassinet. He closed his eyes with a tiny sigh.

Jace held out his hand. She went to him. He turned off the bedroom light, and they headed for the stairs.

In the morning, Jace got up early to take care of a few chores. Tamara lounged in bed until Frankie woke up.

When Jace returned around nine, they hung out at the cabin, doing nothing, really, just being together.

Around eleven, Jace said he would call Sonia, see if she could work for a few hours. He wanted to take Tamara horseback riding.

"I don't know about that," she said. She explained that she'd ridden twice in her life. Once on a trip to Idaho with her mom and one of her mom's boyfriends. And then once not too long ago, with Stephanie and Geoff.

"Geoff put me on a good-natured old horse named Lightning. Lightning, he wasn't. But he was just my speed, meaning he was in no hurry to get anywhere."

"I will introduce you to Dumplin'," Jace promised. "She's sweet as pie and rarely moves faster than a trot."

"Dumplin' sounds like just the horse for me."

But ten seconds later, his fire department pager went off and he had to go. She offered to stay with the baby.

"If you would, just for a bit," he said as he climbed in his crew cab.

"I'm happy to."

"I'll call Sonia on my way, see if she can come on over. If she's unavailable, I'll try my mom. If she can't come, she'll find someone."

"If no one's available, don't worry. I'm here."

"Thank you." He leaned out his window, and she went on tiptoe to kiss him goodbye.

"Be safe," she cautioned.

"Always," he vowed.

Back inside, Frankie was sound asleep. She hung out with the dogs for a bit, and then Sonia appeared. She seemed like a nice woman. Tamara chatted with her a little and then gathered her things to leave.

At home, she did laundry, mopped the kitchen floor and petted her cat.

Jace called in the early evening when he got back to the ranch. She asked about the fire, and he said it was a house fire on the east side of town. The homeowners had left yesterday to visit family in Billings.

"They left a window air conditioner on and plugged into a faulty outlet."

"That's awful, Jace."

"Yeah. The house was gutted, but it was empty, and we got it under control before it spread."

"That's good, at least."

"True. Then we got another call on a brush fire six miles outside of town. Before we got it contained, it burned down a couple of sheds and a stable. Again, nobody was injured, and they got the horses out in time."

"You must be beat."

"I'm fine—and I really want to see you tonight."

She wanted to see him, too. But he needed rest. Reluctantly, she reminded him, "I'm on shift first thing tomorrow morning until seven p.m. And correct me if I'm wrong, but don't you start your round-the-clock shift at the station tomorrow?"

"Yes, I do," he said glumly.

"Tonight, you need to spend a little time with Frankie."

"Okay, okay. You're right. But I miss you."

She teased, "It's only been, what?"

"Ten endless hours," he grumbled.

"Don't be grumpy, Jace."

"Fine. Okay, I get it. I hate it—but I get it. You need your sleep and so do I."

"Exactly."

They talked until the baby demanded his undivided attention. She missed him the moment she said goodbye.

But she went to sleep smiling and got up Sunday morning feeling happy and refreshed.

The day started out just fine, with a first-time mom coming in fully dilated and effaced. Her beautiful, healthy little girl was born two hours later. The mom reached for her baby, and the newborn latched right on to nurse.

Tamara left the birthing suite smiling. She didn't even let it bother her when Eric slithered in beside her at the nurses' station. Instead, she just moved away a bit and reminded herself that she'd really dodged a bullet with that creep. At least he knew better than to actually touch her. And he kept his mouth shut, so that was a bonus, as well.

But then one of the ward clerks asked her a question. As she glanced up to answer, Eric winked at her—after which he lost the smarmy smile and put on a pouty face.

Keeping her expression bland, she turned away. Really, the guy had a problem if he couldn't figure out that the last thing she wanted was attention from him. And did he seriously believe that pretending to pout would be somehow attractive to her?

Not a question she should be wasting any brain space on. She took Taylor Swift's sage advice and shook it off.

But then at lunchtime, she saw Eric in the cafeteria sharing his break with Jeannie Crane, one of the phlebotomists from the lab. They sat at the same table, leaning in close together over their lunch trays. Jeannie was flushed and smiling. Eric wore a permanent smirk. The vibe was downright intimate.

And then, as Tamara walked by on her way outside to join Stephanie, Jeannie said in a whisper loud enough that Tamara heard, "Tonight, then?"

"Don't worry, baby," Eric whispered back. "I'll be there." He had more to say, but by then Tamara was already out the door.

As usual, Stephanie read her like a large-print book. "What's going on?" her friend demanded as Tamara took the other café chair at the small iron table under a cute dwarf maple tree in the courtyard. "Your cheeks are way too pink."

"You don't need to hear it."

"But see, that's where you're wrong."

Tamara went ahead and told her friend what she'd just heard, ending with, "Apparently, my least favorite doctor has moved on from Elise."

Stephanie groaned. "I have to ask. Is it just me or sometimes, don't you kind of feel like a bit player on *Grey's Anatomy*?"

They laughed together over that and then moved on to the subject of Friday night. The four of them, Stephanie and Geoff, and Tamara and Jace, were going to DJ's Deluxe, a great barbecue restaurant in Bronco Heights.

When they left the courtyard to go back to work, Eric and Jeannie were nowhere to be seen. Tamara felt relieved. She'd had more than enough of Dr. Pearce and his womanizing ways for one day.

Too bad that when she entered the staff lounge two hours later, she found Elise showing off her engagement ring to a circle of five eager colleagues. For a split second, Tamara actually thought that maybe Elise had found some other guy after her breakup with Eric.

But then Elise said, "Eric proposed in Vegas. It's been a whirlwind. We flew down Wednesday, had the most glorious two days at the Venetian. And then yesterday, before we flew back, he took me to Tiffany's."

For a moment, Tamara actually felt sorry for Elise.

But only a moment. And then, as the women surrounding Elise oohed and ahhed over the diamond on her finger, Elise spotted Tamara frozen in the doorway to the hall with her mouth hanging open. A triumphant smile curved the red lips of Eric Pearce's new fiancée—on whom he was evidently planning to cheat that very night.

Tamara snapped her mouth shut and walked back out the door. Really, she couldn't believe Eric. What a slimy chum bucket, as her second stepfather, a saltwater fishing enthusiast, had been known to remark.

She reminded herself sternly that Eric cheating on the woman he'd cheated on *her* with was none of her business and that what goes around comes around. At some point, Dr. Pearce's sleazy behavior was bound to catch up with him.

"You saw Elise's engagement ring?" Stephanie asked her at seven fifteen as they left the hospital together.

"Yes, I did." They stood in the parking lot next to Tamara's SUV, and Tamara confessed, "I almost considered clueing in Elise as to Eric's cheating ways."

"Tell me you changed your mind."

"I did, yes."

"Good. I mean, she knew that he was with *you* when *she* slept with him. That should have been all the clueing-in she needed to realize the man cannot be trusted." Stephanie wrapped an arm around Tamara's shoulders. "You're the best. Your instincts are to help, to reach out, because you are a truly sweet person."

"Don't call me sweet."

"It's not an insult."

"I know, but… Sometimes I think that when it comes to men, my judgment is just plain bad. How could I have thought that I loved a man like Eric Pearce? Clearly, I'm messed up when it comes to men. My romantic instincts suck. I don't know what I'm doing, and it always ends in disaster."

"Wrong."

"Stephanie, Eric was the worst of the worst. You know he was."

"Can't argue with that. But come on. You're figuring out the relationship thing just fine now. Jace is a great guy."

"That's true," Tamara agreed. Because he was.

"So put the dark thoughts away. You've found a wonderful man and life is good."

Things really had been going well. She should focus on that, push all her negative doubts and fears away. "You're right," she said. "It is good with Jace. Really good."

"That's better." Her friend gave her another side hug and let her go. They chatted for a minute or two more and then Stephanie headed for her own car.

At home, Tamara ate some leftover pasta for dinner and then retired to the bathroom for a long soak in the tub. She wanted to call Jace, but he would be at the station now—or maybe even out on a call. She didn't want to disturb him at work, even if she did long for the sound of his voice.

And truthfully now, wasn't she getting in too deep, too quickly with Jace?

Yes, she'd agreed with Stephanie earlier, that things were good between her and Jace. But they'd known each other less than a month. And already, she wanted to spend every spare moment with him. Already, she was planning how well his dogs and her cat would get along, imagining a life with him and Frankie, the three of them making a family together on the Bonnie B.

Maybe all the hospital drama around her ex ought to be a wake-up call for her. It hadn't been very long since she'd ended it with Eric, and yet here she was, spinning fantasies about a future with Jace.

The more she thought about the situation, the more she realized that she needed to slow things down with him. Instead of racing to his side every chance she got, she needed to back off a little, see him once or twice a week, tops, for a while.

She stared at the tiled wall above the tub faucet, feeling suddenly sad and strangely bereft. Because she didn't want to see him less.

On the contrary, she wanted to be with him constantly.

And that was dangerous. Foolish.

Space. That was what she really needed. He had Frankie now. He didn't have to worry that some young couple would swoop in and adopt the baby. He just didn't need Tamara as much as he had in those first frantic weeks, as he worked to get certified as a foster parent. He even had a nanny now to help him look after the little boy.

She settled back into her froth of bubbles, rested her head on a thick towel and wished she didn't feel so miserable about her decision.

Not far away, she heard Harley's loud purr.

When she glanced toward the sound, he was sitting right there in the open doorway, amber eyes at half-mast, watching her.

"Staring is rude," she reminded him.

He just kept on purring.

"Well, you might as well be the first to know. I'm going to pull away from Jace a little, give us both some room to breathe. I think it will be a good thing for both of us. And I'm giving him his house key back. It's way too early for me to have a key."

Harley didn't comment—but then he never did. As a rule, that was part of the joy of talking to him. She could wrestle with her issues out loud without any interruptions to her thought process.

Tonight, though, the more she talked about putting distance between her and Jace, the more unsettled she felt.

Well, too bad. She knew she'd made the right decision and she was sticking with it.

The next day she was scheduled to work ten to six. As she ate breakfast, she obsessed over the plan she'd hatched in the tub the night before.

The thing was, she didn't *want* to do it. She didn't want to pull away from Jace. She wanted to be with him every single chance she got.

Which meant she needed to get this over with before she backed down, needed to act now rather than later. She'd go see him this morning before she headed for the hospital. Once she'd told him she needed some space, she would feel better. She could get back to life as usual, get a little balance, achieve a better sense of...

What, exactly?

She set down her coffee mug sharply.

Who was she kidding?

She *cared* for Jace. And for Frankie, too. She wanted to be with Jace. And the worst thing she could do right now—the most cowardly, self-destructive thing—would be to give him his key back and demand some space.

Uh-uh.

Last night, she'd let her fears and misgivings take charge.

In the clear light of day, she saw how wrong she'd been.

She had to step up, she really did. It was time to draw the line on herself and her wimpy, self-sabotaging doubts. Time to refuse to let the bad behavior of disappointing men tarnish her relationship with the good man she'd finally found.

Tamara turned to her cat, who sat on the floor five

feet from her chair, purring as usual. "I'm driving to the Bonnie B this morning," she informed Harley firmly. "Jace should be there sometime between seven thirty and eight. I'm going to tell him I only have a few minutes and I have to get to work, but that I just wanted to see him first. And then I'm going to grab him and plant one on him, just so he knows that I want to be with him and I'm not afraid of that."

Harley purred louder. She decided to take that as a sign that he agreed with everything she'd just said.

It was a little after eight when Tamara pulled up in front of Jace's cabin. His truck was there—and Bonnie's Jeep, too. Either Jace's mom had stayed the night to watch the baby, or she'd come over earlier in the morning for some reason or other. Her presence threw a wrench in Tamara's plan to get a private moment with Jace.

Well, so what? She'd driven out here and she wanted to see him, however briefly. And even if she had to hold off on that smoking hot kiss because his mother was there, he would still know that she'd taken the long way to work in order to get a few minutes with him.

As she walked up the front steps, she could hear voices inside. It had been a nice night and the front windows were open.

At the door, just as she raised her hand to knock,

she heard Bonnie say, "You know I'm right. Why are you dragging your heels?"

"Stop, Mom."

"No. Uh-uh. Not until I know you're listening. Because you need to marry Tamara. That will get the adoption on a fast track. I can guarantee you that."

Tamara waited, hand still raised, not even breathing, for Jace to announce that he would never marry her—or anyone—just to get permanent custody of Frankie. That marriage was a sacred trust that required mutual love and respect.

Or something like that.

But he didn't say what she yearned to hear. Instead, he announced flatly, "Don't worry, Mom. I'm on it."

Bonnie spoke again, more quietly than before and in a coaxing tone. Tamara couldn't make out the words.

Not that it mattered.

She'd heard more than enough and just wanted to get out of there. But as she started to turn for her car, she froze.

Running away? No. She absolutely refused to do that.

Drawing herself up to her full almost-five feet, she knocked.

The voices inside stopped. Firm steps approached the door.

Jace pulled the door wide and a giant smile spread

over his face. He really did seem happy to see her. "Hey." He stepped back. "Come on in." He said over his shoulder, loud enough so his mom could hear, "My mom's here, but I promise you she's just leaving."

"Tamara, hi!" Bonnie came toward them, Bailey and Luna at her heels. "I'm just on my way back to the house."

"Hi, Bonnie." Tamara pasted on a smile and bent to give each dog a quick pat. "How're you doing?"

"Just great." Bonnie squeezed her son's arm. "Think about what I said."

He kissed the top of Bonnie's head. "Bye, Mom."

"I'm going, I'm going." With a final wave, Bonnie went down the steps.

"Come in." Jace ushered her forward.

She stepped into the entry hall and heard Bonnie start up her Jeep as Jace shut the door. He gave her a long, slow once-over, from her pulled-back hair to her blue scrubs and all the way down to her comfy work shoes. Her breath hitched uncomfortably as he met her eyes again.

Because it hurt, what she'd heard, what she knew she had to do now.

Her sudden change of heart this morning had been wishful thinking, pure and simple. Her original plan was the right one. Her silly fantasy of forever with Jace was over. Now she just needed to rip the emotional bandage off and get back to her real life.

Jace was frowning now. "What's wrong? What's

happened?" The dogs stared up at her. Bailey let out a low, worried whine.

She drew a breath through her nose. "I'm on my way to work, but I wonder if I could have a few minutes?"

"Hey..." He started to reach for her, but when she put up both hands he let his arms drop to his sides. "Are you all right?"

She backed up a step. "Um. No, Jace. Not really."

"Come on in the main room," he said, his voice carefully even, as he gestured for her to go ahead of him.

She perched on a chair. "Is Frankie still sleeping?"

"Yeah." The dogs stood nearby, watching them, their heads turning back and forth between the two of them. Luna made a sound—a whine of concern. "Lie down," he said to both of them. They flopped to the rug. He sat on the end of the sofa. "Talk to me."

"I've, uh, been thinking..." She tried to compose her thoughts. He sat there across from her, his eyes stormy, his mouth a bleak line, as though he already knew what she planned to say. But she had to give him credit. He waited for her to say it. "This has all happened fast, that's all. Too fast for me. And I'm not that long out of a really bad relationship. Your life is packed, with essentially two jobs and a baby son. The, uh, timing is bad for both of us, surely you can see that."

"No, Tamara. I can't see it. The timing seems just

right to me. So will you please tell me what's really going on here? Tell me the truth, whatever it is. Tell me what's bothering you."

"I just need to move on."

He sat straighter. "You need to…?"

"I think you heard me. I said I need to move on."

He asked in a near whisper, "What are you doing?"

"I just told you. It's over."

"Come on, Tamara. This isn't like you. You would never dump me for no reason."

"But I'm not…" She caught herself. Because she was dumping him. He wanted her for Frankie's sake. That would never be enough for her. "Look. I just gave you a reason. More than one."

He shook his head. "I don't buy those reasons. Uh-uh. Just tell me the truth about what's *really* bothering you. Talk to me honestly. Where is this coming from?"

"From me, Jace." She slid her small purse off her shoulder and reached in the front pocket to pull out his house key, which she set on the coffee table between them. "I have to get to work." She started to rise.

He held her in place with a look. "Just like that, you're done with me, with us?"

"Yes, I… Jace, look. It's just not working for me."

He tipped his head to the side, eyes narrowing. "Why not? What's happened that made it suddenly stop working?"

She threw up both hands. "What do you want me to say?"

"The truth. That's what I want. It's *all* I want."

She went ahead and gave it to him. "Well, I just don't need a man who has ulterior motives for being with me. I really don't."

"Ulterior…" He was scowling now. And then his eyes went wide. "Wait. Okay. The windows are open. And you heard what my mother said."

"I, um…"

"Just say it. You did hear what my mother said." He waited for her answer. When she failed to give him one, he shook his head. "You heard her say I should marry you to get Frankie, and you heard me answer that I'm on it."

Why was she holding back? She tipped up her chin. "Yes, I heard both of those things."

"And you believe that about me—that I would trick you into marrying me just to make sure the adoption goes through?"

Did she? Really? "Okay, it doesn't seem like something you would do."

"You're right. I wouldn't do it. What you heard was just my mom matchmaking us because she thinks the world of you and she wants us together permanently. Which is exactly what I want, too, just in case you haven't figured that out yet."

"You want us together—forever?"

"I do. And as for my answer to my mother, I said I

was 'on it' to back her off, plain and simple. I wanted her to butt out because it's not her business. What happens with you and me, that's for you and me to decide."

Her breath was all tangled up in her chest. "But you didn't tell her you would never marry someone just to get Frankie."

He closed his eyes and shook his head. "I didn't *need* to tell her. She already knows." But then he looked at her again, so steadily, like the good, direct, honest man he was. "I can see, though, that *you* need to hear it. Tamara, I would never marry you—or anyone—just to get custody of Frankie. That would be wrong. I don't operate like that."

Longing moved through her, an ache and a promise. It was all this talk of marriage messing with her, tempting her to imagine having Jace for a husband, the two of them loving each other, equally dedicated to raising Frankie together.

But who was she kidding? All that was just her own sad, unfulfilled fantasies talking. Even if she could believe in him, she didn't really believe in herself. Just look at her now. Making a mess of everything. A human yo-yo of conflicting emotions.

She was an excellent friend and a fine nurse. She had a kind heart and she cared for others. But her romantic history proved that she was just better off on her own, that her absent father and her mother's screwed up priorities had damaged her when it came to finding love and forever. And she needed to face that, to learn to live with that.

"Jace, it isn't only what I heard through the window a few minutes ago. I really have started thinking about this, about us. I've started thinking that I'm not ready for anything serious with a man. I'm really not. I just can't do this thing with you anymore, that's all. I'm only messing it up, and that's not good for either of us." She stood and settled her purse strap on her shoulder. "Goodbye."

He rose, too. They faced off across the coffee table and he asked, "Is this about that scumbag doctor who cheated on you?"

She gasped. "I never said he was a doctor."

"Oh, come on, Tamara. It's Bronco. People talk. And Eric Pearce has made a name for himself—and not only as an excellent doctor. He's also got a rep as a real piece of work. Word is he's plowed his way through several of the women on Bronco Valley Hospital's staff. I am not him."

"I know you're not. I never, ever thought you were."

"Well, that's something, I guess."

"I, um, I do have to go now."

He braced his strong legs apart and folded his powerful arms across his chest. "You're really pissing me off, Tamara. You know that?" He spoke harshly. It was so unlike him.

And that broke her heart all over again, that she'd

pushed a kind and thoughtful man like him to the point of bitterness. "Oh, Jace. It can't work with us. I can't do this. I just don't have the trust it takes to try again, to give my heart to you and count on you not to break it."

He gave her a one-shouldered shrug. "You've got no idea how bad I want to try to stop you, to beg you to see that all you have to do is stay, talk to me, work it out with me."

"But I can't stay. I really can't—oh, Jace, I'm sorry. I truly am. I'm just not in a good place to build a relationship—and I really do need to go now."

He said nothing for several awful seconds. Finally, he shook his head. "I don't know what more to say to you. It's pretty damn clear you've made up your mind." Those beautiful eyes of his accused her of being a coward, of running away.

Because she was, on both counts.

"Goodbye, Jace." She turned and started walking.

He made no attempt to stop her—and that was good, she reassured herself. She didn't want him to stop her.

She went out the door and straight to her car. Sliding in behind the wheel, she started the engine and headed for town.

Her eyes welled with tears. She swiped them away and focused on the road ahead.

It was over with Jace, and it hurt really bad to

leave him behind, to turn her back on sweet little Frankie.

But eventually in life, a woman had to come to grips with her own limitations. She'd done the right thing, she promised herself. Jace and Frankie were better off without her.

And in time, she was going to be okay.

Chapter Eleven

Jace sat on the sofa with his elbows braced on his spread knees and his head between his hands. He heard Tamara's car start up and drive away.

She'd been gone for maybe five minutes when the front door opened. "Jace?"

He drew a deep, slow breath. "Not now, Mom!"

Unfortunately, for Bonnie Abernathy, boundaries were only pesky obstacles for her to bust right through. She came marching into the living area and loomed above him. "Tamara's gone already? That was fast. Is everything okay?"

He sat up straight and looked her square in the eye. "I'll say it again, more clearly this time. I would like to be alone right now."

Bonnie blinked. "Something happened. What?"

He threw up both hands. "She says it's over."

"What? I don't get it. Why? You were so happy together, and now suddenly she breaks it off?"

"Just go on home, Mom. Please?"

She dropped into the chair Tamara had been sitting in just minutes before. "Okay, I did see that look on her face..."

"Go home, Mom. You've done enough."

"I... What is that supposed to mean?"

He went ahead and told her. "The front windows were wide open. She heard what you said, that I should marry her to speed up the adoption. And she heard what I said, too."

His mom gasped. "Oh, no! So, then she's completely misconstrued the situation and she's hurt, and I don't blame her!"

"Just... Look, that's not it."

"Not it? Not what? I don't understand what you're saying."

"What I'm saying is, we hashed that out, Tamara and me. What she overheard this morning upset her but it's not the real issue."

"She said that?"

"Yes. And I believe her."

"Then what *is* the real issue?"

"Mom. Let it be. This is not about you."

Her face crumpled. "You're right. But still. Oh, honey. Me and my big mouth. I'm so sorry. I promise I'll make it right."

"Stay out of it, Mom. I mean it."

"But if I were to—"

"Don't even think about it. This is about Tamara and me. I'm asking you not to get in the middle of it."

"But you just let her go…"

"Of course I did. What? I should have held her here against her will?"

Now his mom looked outraged. "I didn't say that. But you do need to go after her, honey. You really do." Now her eyes filled with tears. "Oh, honey, I'm so sorry."

"Mom." Rising, he stepped around the coffee table to drop to a crouch in front of her, as she pulled a tissue from her pocket and dabbed at her wet cheeks. "Look at me." He waited until she'd lowered the tissue and met his eyes. "Stop beating up on yourself and let it go."

"But, Jace, I…" Her words trailed off as the first fussy little cry erupted from the baby monitor on the coffee table. "I'll get him."

Jace caught her hands between his. "No. I'll see to him."

She sniffled. "I just feel that I should do *something*."

"I know you do, but there really is nothing you can do right now."

His mom sighed. "All right."

He stood and pulled her up with him. "It's going to be okay," he said as he hugged her.

"You're just trying to get rid of me now."

He almost smiled. "You figured that out, did you?"

"Oh, fine." She pulled away. "I'm going. Let me know if you need anything."

"I will. But right now, I want some time with my son. And after that, I need to think this thing through."

When she got to the hospital, Tamara went straight to the women's room in the staff lounge. For once, there was no one else in there. She took advantage of the rare moment of privacy to splash cold water on her tear-swollen eyes and retouch her minimal makeup.

"There you are!" Stephanie spotted her as she emerged from the restroom. Her friend grabbed her hand and pulled her out of the lounge and into the nearest supply closet.

"What's going on?" Tamara demanded.

"I thought you'd never get here. You know how I said it was *Grey's Anatomy* around here half the time? Well, today we're all the way into *St. Elsewhere* territory. You won't believe what went down."

It did feel kind of good to have hospital gossip to focus on. "Tell me."

"Elise had a meltdown in the cafeteria at seven this morning. She turned the air blue with the things she said to her former fiancé."

"Former? She broke up with Eric?"

"Oh, did she ever. She called him a two-timing, scum-sucking dirty dog and threw that giant diamond in his face. Then she and Jeannie Crane got into it. There was actual hair pulling. They had to call security to settle them down. Then they all three had a meeting with HR, the medical director and various and sundry higher-ups. After that, Dr. Pearce, Elise and Jeannie left the building. Nobody knows yet if any of them are coming back."

"Wow. I honestly never thought it would come to this."

"I know, right?" Stephanie frowned and peered closer at Tamara. "Have you been crying?" Before Tamara could decide how to answer that, her friend figured it out. "Did something happen with Jace?"

The last thing she wanted to do was get into that right now.

Stephanie seemed to understand without even having to be told. "What time are you off?"

"Six."

"I've got the long shift, till seven. I'll come straight to your house. Don't argue. I'll be there." Stephanie grabbed her in a hug, then held her at arm's length. "You going to be okay until tonight?"

She nodded and promised, "I'll survive."

The day was a busy one. Tamara didn't leave the hospital till seven thirty. At home, she'd barely had time to feed Harley and change into shorts and a T-shirt before Stephanie arrived with a pizza to share.

She held it up on one hand and asked, "Why am I getting the feeling our double date Friday night is not going to happen?"

"Sorry," Tamara said softly. "Come on in." She led her friend to the kitchen, where Stephanie put down the pizza and grabbed Tamara in a hug.

A few minutes later, as Tamara opened them a bottle of Chianti, Stephanie instructed, "Tell me everything."

By the time they'd eaten and settled on the sofa, Tamara had told the whole sad story and Stephanie was shaking her head. "You need to call the man. Tell him you got cold feet but you're better now. Just come right out with it. Tell him you love him, and it scares you to death, but you're ready to deal with your fear now. Be as brave as you really are inside."

"But, Stephanie, I'm *not* ready. I don't think I'll ever be."

Her friend was silent. Then she said softly, "Jace Abernathy is not Eric Pearce."

"No, he's not. But still. I chose Eric, and it wasn't all that long ago. After all the drama that's gone down the past couple of days—with Elise and Jeannie and that sleazeball—I can't believe I was with that guy. It makes me seriously doubt my own judgment."

"I get it. I do. But almost everyone gets fooled by love at least once in their lives."

"Well, I got fooled more than once."

"And that is not rare. It's okay to get fooled. It means you're willing to put your heart on the line, that you took a chance on what makes life worthwhile. It's on Eric Pearce that it all blew apart with him. But look at it this way. He did you a favor and showed you who he really was fairly early in the game."

"It didn't feel like a favor."

"I do hear you. I just don't want you to throw away something really good because of a jerk like Eric Pearce. Sheesh. Talk about letting the bad guys win."

Tamara held up the half-empty bottle of wine. "More?"

"Not tonight." They were both on duty at seven tomorrow.

When Tamara walked her friend to the door, she promised to think about what Stephanie had said.

And she did think about it. She thought about it that night when she found it hard to sleep, and she thought about it the next day, too, especially when she learned that neither Eric Pearce nor Elise Wayne would be coming back to Bronco Valley Hospital. Word was they'd both quit.

But whatever had really happened, it was heaven to realize she wouldn't have to deal with either of them again. Jeannie Crane came to work but stayed in the lab all day.

Really, all the staff seemed somewhat subdued.

At lunch in the courtyard, Stephanie said, "Sometimes you don't realize you've been working in a toxic environment until the ones making all the trouble are gone."

For the first time since she'd walked away from Jace, Tamara cracked a smile—a small one, but still. "It does feel different around here—less tense, less dangerous, somehow."

Stephanie agreed. "We got lucky. The bad guys just packed up and left." She raised her iced macchiato, and Tamara tapped it with her bottle of Hint water.

That evening at home, Tamara cooked herself a simple dinner, ate it, cleaned up the kitchen and then put on sleep shorts and a giant T-shirt. She was happy about the reduced emotional turmoil at work, but at home, well, she missed Jace. She wondered how Frankie was doing.

To distract herself from thoughts of what might have been, she climbed into bed and tried to get lost in a thriller she'd started a few days before.

After reading the same page three times running, she accepted the fact that her concentration was out the window. Out the window and up the highway a few miles at the Bonnie B.

With Jace and Frankie.

She tossed the book aside, disturbing Harley, who

got up, stretched and left the bed. "Sorry to bother you," she called after him sourly.

He strutted on out into the hallway, black tail held high.

She flopped back against her pillow and scowled into the middle distance. Nothing felt right tonight. Nothing at all. She was lonely and out of sorts and wished—

Well, it didn't matter what she wished.

She and Jace were through. Period. End of story.

When her phone buzzed with a text, she almost didn't check it.

But then she picked it up, punched in her pin, brought up the text app and saw it was from Jace. I heard a rumor.

Suddenly breathless, she stared at the screen. And then her fingers were flying. A rumor about what?

That Dr. Eric Pearce no longer works at Bronco Valley Hospital.

Grinning maniacally at the phone, she wrote, Well, you heard right.

She hit send and then watched the little text bubbles bouncing, disappearing—and then bouncing again. Her heart threatened to stage a breakout from the cage of her chest.

And then finally, his response came through. Frankie and I are coming over.

She let out a squeak of surprise, pressed her hand

to her chest where her poor heart kept racing—and then typed, No!

What she did not do was hit send. Instead, she stared at that one word for at least thirty seconds, after which she deleted it and wrote, like a complete wimp, You shouldn't.

His response was instantaneous. We're on our way.

She wrote and deleted five different responses. In all of them, she firmly insisted that he *not* come over.

Somehow, she just couldn't bring herself to send a single one of the five.

So she tossed the phone on the nightstand, jumped from the bed and stuck her feet in her favorite pink flip-flops.

Out in the kitchen, she grabbed last night's half bottle of wine from the counter, pulled out the cork and knocked back a big gulp of it—which was ridiculous. Did she think getting drunk would fix anything? She stuck the cork back in the bottle and went out to the living room to wait.

After the longest twenty minutes of her life, she heard his truck pull up out front.

Jumping to her feet, she marched to the door, threw it wide and strode across the porch, down the steps and along her front walk, her flip-flops slapping her feet with each step.

Jace's window slid down when she reached it.

"Hey," he said in that voice of his that turned her knees to mush.

She tried to be firm. "What are you doing here?"

He tipped his head to the side, frowning, considering his reply. And then he said, "Showing up."

"What does that mean?" she snapped—but in a whisper, because she could see the shadowed shape of Frankie's car seat in back. The baby was sleeping, his little head drooping to the side, like a big flower on a slender stalk. She didn't want to wake him.

Jace whispered, "I've been thinking that a lot of caring about someone is really just showing up. Being there. I care about you. So here I am."

"I said you shouldn't come."

"*Shouldn't.* That's not the same as saying, *Jace, I don't want you here,* now is it?"

"I don't know what you're going on about."

"I think you do. I think you're afraid, and that's okay. I get it. Because no man has ever really shown up for you." He scowled. "I hate that those bastards did that to you." His eyes gleamed and his scowl tipped into a half smile. "But if they hadn't been schmucks, I wouldn't be getting my shot with you, now, would I?"

The things he said sometimes...

They made her feel warm all over. They made the tears rise in her eyes—the good kind of tears. The dangerous kind, too. Because they had hope in them.

She tried her best to steel herself against that silver tongue of his. "You should go home, Jace. Put Frankie to bed."

"You plan on inviting me in?"

"It's a bad idea."

"Well, then I guess I'll just sit right here for a while if that's okay with you."

"What for?"

He looked at her so tenderly. "For you. In case you decide you might have something you need to say to me."

"Like what?"

"Well, I won't know until you say it, will I?"

"You are making no sense at all. I'm just going inside."

"All right, then. Good night, Tamara."

She turned on her heel and marched back to the house, feeling equal parts giddy and self-righteous as she silently shut and locked the door behind her. Turning, she saw Harley sitting on the sofa across the room, watching her.

She grumbled, "What are you looking at?" He started purring and diligently cleaning one of his back paws. "Whatever. I'm going back to bed."

Flip-flops flapping, she turned off the lights and went back to her room, where she switched off the bedside lamp, stretched out under the covers and closed her eyes.

It didn't help. No way could she sleep. Because she was expending way too much energy listening for the sound of Jace's truck starting up and driving away.

Twenty-five minutes crawled by—she knew how much time had passed because she kept checking it on her phone, the screen lighting up too brightly in the dark bedroom.

Finally, with a ridiculous, overly loud "Argh!" she threw back the covers, shoved on her flip-flops and flapped back out to his truck.

He opened the window as she approached the driver's door. "Everything okay?"

"Don't you have to do some ranching stuff in the morning?"

"I do. Don't worry about me, though. Frankie and I will get home in time."

"You're just going to sit out here until you have to get back to the ranch?"

"Yeah, that's my plan."

She folded her arms across her middle. "No. Uh-uh. No. It's just not right."

He looked at her sideways, a frown drawing down between his brows. "What's not right, exactly?"

"Well, sleeping in your crew cab all night. That can't be comfortable. And the baby—"

"Tamara, we're fine."

She scoffed, "If you're determined to stay the night here, you'd better come inside."

His slow smile almost undid her. "Yeah?"

"You can sleep in the guest room."

"That'll work."

"What about diapers and formula?"

"I have everything he needs and an overnight bag for myself with a shaving kit, toothbrush, clean shirt, the works."

She braced her hands on her hips. "You know this is ridiculous, right?"

He just kept on looking at her like he couldn't get enough of the sight of her.

Five minutes later, she held the sleeping baby as he set up a soft-sided travel bassinet beside the guest room bed.

"Okay," he whispered. "It's ready."

Carefully, she set the little sweetheart in his travel bed. "He looks so peaceful." She glanced up and found Jace watching her. "What?"

"Just so you know, I'll be back tomorrow night."

"You're not serious."

"Oh, yeah, I am. I'll be here a lot."

"But it's inconvenient for you."

"A little maybe. But think of all the times you came out to the ranch, inconveniencing yourself to help me and Frankie out."

"Oh. So you *owe* me somehow?"

"I do, yeah. But that's not what I meant. I meant that you're not coming out to the ranch anymore. So if I want to be around you, I have to go where you are. Also, I was wondering if maybe you could just let me borrow a key."

She had to stifle a laugh. "Oh, Jace."

"Because Frankie and I have to leave at four thirty or so, and I really don't want to wake you up, but I'm not leaving you with your front door unlocked. So it's a problem. Maybe I should just go on back out to the truck." His eyes were kind of glowing now, all soft and full of promises she kept trying to tell herself she couldn't afford to believe.

She accused, "You have no shame."

"Not when it comes to you."

They had a mini staring contest, which he won when she heard herself sigh. "Fine. I'll get you a key." She went out to the kitchen, grabbed a spare key from the utility drawer and returned to the guest room, where he was sitting on the edge of the bed, waiting.

She handed him the key, her fingers brushing his warm palm, the contact sending a riot of delicious little shivers dancing up the back of her arm. "Happy now?"

"Getting there."

She turned and left him, heading straight for her bed, all too aware that she could have easily sent him away if she'd wanted to. A clear command would have done it. *Leave. I don't want you here.*

Six little words. But she hadn't said them.

Instead, she'd said how he *shouldn't* come to her house, how he'd better come in if he wasn't going to leave. Now she'd probably toss and turn all night, berating herself for all the wrong signals she shouldn't be giving him—including handing him her house key, for crying out loud.

Surprisingly, she went right to sleep, waking only once at a little after midnight when she heard Frankie cry.

A minute later, she heard Jace's voice, deep and soothing, though she couldn't quite make out what he said. She shut her eyes and sleep settled over her again.

When she got up at six, Jace and Frankie were gone. The guest room bed was neatly made, the empty travel bassinet waiting beside it.

She smiled at the sight of that bassinet.

Guess he really was planning on showing up again tonight.

Out in the courtyard during lunch, she told Stephanie everything.

Her friend let out a gleeful laugh. "Oh, that Jace Abernathy. The man's got game. I like his style."

"I can't believe I gave him a key."

Stephanie leaned across the little iron table. "Just give in," she whispered. "You know you will eventually, anyway. Let yourself be happy."

"I don't know what I'm doing. I really don't."

"Are you going to ask for that key back?"

"Well, I, uh…"

Stephanie only smiled.

* * *

Jace got to Tamara's house at six thirty that evening. She usually got off at seven, so he was early.

He waited outside for her, with Frankie. He didn't want to push her boundaries too hard or make assumptions. After all, he'd asked for the key so that he could leave without waking her—not so he could get in when she wasn't home.

She pulled in at seven fifteen, jumped out of her little SUV and came straight to the pickup, where she leaned in the open window. "You hungry?"

He tried not to smile *too* wide. "Always."

"Bring Frankie and all your stuff in. Dinner's in half an hour."

A kiss.

Tamara couldn't stop thinking about how much she wanted one.

It was after nine. She sat on the sofa with Jace. Harley had taken the easy chair. As for Frankie, he'd dropped off to sleep a few minutes ago. Jace had let her put him to bed in his guest room bassinet.

And Tamara knew she needed to do some serious talking before she could start pushing for kisses.

She reached for his hand. He gave it, lifting her hand to his warm lips and brushing a kiss across her knuckles.

"I don't know where to start," she said. "I can't see any reason why you should believe me right now if I say how much I care about you. How much I want you."

He raised her hand to his lips again. His breath was warm on her skin. "Gotta say, I really like where this is going."

"Oh, Jace. You shouldn't trust me."

"Hey." He wrapped his arm around her and pulled her into his broad, strong chest. She leaned against him. "I do trust you," he said. She felt his lips brush the crown of her head. She wanted to melt right into him, to sit here, cradled in his big arms, until morning came. "Tamara, you've been hurt and hurt again. You can take as long as you need to learn to trust me, to believe that I will never let you down."

"I do believe it." She tipped her head back to capture his gaze. "And I realize that it's so unfair of me to keep pushing you away. The other day, when I left you at the ranch, I was sure you would never let me near you again. I tried to tell myself that was good, that it was what I wanted. But inside, Jace... Inside, I was dying."

"Sweetheart." He brushed a kiss across her lips. "Yeah, I was mad at you the other day. Real mad."

"And I don't blame you. I hurt you. I'm so sorry."

He granted her another soft and perfect kiss. "You are forgiven."

"I'm a hot mess," she confessed, "wanting to be with you, getting cold feet, telling you that friendship is all that I want, even breaking it off with you the way I did Monday. And then, here you are, trying again, busting down my defenses, filling my heart so I never, ever want to let you go."

He chuckled and kissed her forehead. She snuggled in close once more. "That's my plan," he said. "To find the ways to bust through every one of your defenses." His voice was a rough rumble in her ear. "I'm really pleased to hear you say that my plan is working."

She said honestly, "I don't want to get rid of you. I never did. But after all the disappointments before I found you, my fears have overridden the longing in my heart. And when I heard your mom and you through the window the other morning..."

"I get it. What else were you to think but that you'd been fooled again? I can't blame you for being cautious, I honestly can't. Right now, it's my job to show you that I'm here, that it's real between us, that we really can work it out."

She laid her hand against his cheek. "Right now, you should kiss me."

He smiled at that. "I aim to please." His wonderful mouth touched hers.

She sighed and snuggled closer, opening to him joyfully. He kissed her deeply and she promised herself that this time she would not pull away.

A little while later, she whispered, "Let's go to my room."

He took her hand and scooped up the baby monitor from the coffee table.

In her bedroom, he undressed her slowly, almost reverently. When he pulled her down onto the bed with him, she went eagerly. Pulling him closer, shewhispered his name.

"Don't go," she grumbled when he climbed from the bed. It was almost five in the morning.

He bent close and kissed her cheek. "There's work to do on the Bonnie B. Ranch work waits for no man. Frankie and I will be back tonight."

She wrapped her arms around his neck. "I'm getting really spoiled, having you here waiting when I get home."

"I like you spoiled. It suits you." He kissed the space between her brows. "Okay if I let myself in tonight?"

"Please do."

"I'll bring takeout."

She smiled against his warm lips. "Yes, please. I clock out at six tonight. Then Friday and Saturday I'm off."

"Come out to the ranch with me tomorrow and stay over. I need to take you horseback riding."

"I would love to."

One more kiss and he left her. Sometime after he tiptoed from the room and quietly closed the door behind him, she drifted back to sleep.

* * *

At Bronco Valley Hospital, the day sped by.

She and Stephanie had lunch in the courtyard. Her friend was thrilled that she was working things out with Jace. They decided to reschedule dinner at DJ's Deluxe for the first Friday in August.

It was a quiet workday overall, with only one baby born during Tamara's shift. She had one preemie in the NICU, but the little guy was doing well. Her supervisor let her check out at five.

Tamara drove home smiling, thinking about the night to come—until she pulled up in front of her house and spotted her mom sitting on the front porch with six Louis Vuitton suitcases standing guard on either side of her slim, designer-clad form. Apparently, she planned to stay a while.

Chapter Twelve

"Darling." Olivia rose as Tamara started up the steps. "At last."

Tamara tried to decide which question to ask first. She settled on a weak remark that wasn't a question at all. "This is a surprise."

"I'm so glad to see you!" Her mom reached for a hug.

Tamara slid between the suitcases and into her mom's arms. They were the same height, but Tamara had to look up. Olivia was wearing six-inch heels.

When Olivia released her, she asked, "Mom, what's going on?"

Her mom waved a perfectly manicured hand. "Can we just go inside first, please? I've been sitting here for over an hour."

Tamara tried really hard not to let her exasperation show as she replied very sweetly, "You realize you didn't call and I had no idea that you were coming."

"You're right." Olivia nodded tightly. "I should have called. Now, can we *please* go in?"

Tamara unlocked the door. Harley waited on the other side, ready to make a run for it as always.

Tamara scooped him up. "No, you don't, Mr. Sneaky." She nuzzled his furry neck, and he purred with contentment.

Behind her, Olivia made an impatient sound.

Tamara turned to her. "I'll just put him in my room."

Her mom drew a slow breath, as though trying really hard to contain her irritation. "Good idea."

Tamara put the cat in the bedroom, and they wheeled all the bags inside and back to the guest room. That took a few minutes.

As Tamara rolled in the last one, she found her mother standing by the bed, frowning at Frankie's bassinet. "Darling. Is there a baby sleeping in here?"

"Yes. Remember I told you that Jace is in the process of adopting a baby named Frankie?"

"Jace. Right. The cowboy firefighter."

That did it. Tamara demanded, "What is going on with you? The last time we talked, you were so rude and mean-spirited, I practically hung up on you. You haven't called to apologize. Instead, you just show up out of nowhere with enough luggage for a cruise around the world and behave as though you can barely control your annoyance at me and my cat and a wonderful man you haven't even met yet."

The most bizarre thing happened then. Her mother's lip started quivering. She looked as though she might burst into tears. And Olivia Smith Hanson De-Leon Arbuckle Atkinson never surrendered to tears.

"Mom? What's the matter? Are you—"

"I'm sorry, all right?" Olivia sobbed. Tears overflowed her lower lids and trickled down her cheeks. She whipped a handkerchief from her Birkin bag and dabbed at her streaming eyes. "I'm sorry for what I said on the phone and for being impatient and rude just now. I'm a terrible bitch and I know it, and I think Nigel has left me, and I'm going to end up all alone with no one to love me—not even you because I'm so mean all the time even my only daughter refuses to put up with me."

All of Tamara's frustration and annoyance drained away as though it had never been. "Oh, Mom…"

Olivia sniffled. "What?" she asked sharply.

Tamara pulled her close and patted her slim, straight back. "It's okay, Mom."

"No, it's not. It is most definitely *not* okay." She sniffled some more, then pulled away to wipe at her eyes again. "I honestly am sorry for the things I said about your new guy. And I did come here planning to tell you so, but then, well, you know how I am. I open my mouth and snotty things come out."

Tamara took her hands, led her around the bassinet and pulled her down to the side of the bed. "Mom, I will always love you, no matter what. No, I won't put up with you sniping at me and saying cruel things about Jace or innocent little Frankie. But that doesn't mean I don't love you."

Her mom let out a sad little sob. "Oh, you are much too good a person to have been raised by me."

Tamara pulled her close again. "I've never seen you like this. Is this because of Nigel?" Always before when one of her mom's marriages was on the rocks, Olivia had been cool, determined and ready to move on.

"Oh, I don't know what has happened to me. I must be getting weak in my old age."

"Mom. You're fifty-five. We all know fifty is the new thirty."

Her mom dabbed at her eyes some more. "We do?"

"Absolutely."

Olivia blew her nose. "Well, it's good to know I'm younger than I thought, but still. Oh, darling. I'm in love with my husband, and I'm afraid he doesn't love me anymore."

Tamara tried to get her mom to explain what had actually happened with Nigel. Olivia just said he was always away on a business trip. "He doesn't want to be with me. Tamara, he's always gone."

"Does he know you're here?"

"I have no idea. He was still off in Vegas when I headed for the airport."

"Did you leave him a note at least?"

"Oh, yes, I did. A mean note—the kind someone like me might write. And you know what? Right now, I just want to unpack a few things and maybe take a long, hot bath." She framed Tamara's face between her soft hands. "I love you so much, my darling. Having you was the best thing I ever did. Somehow, you grew up good and kind and always doing the right thing and helping others. I have no idea how that happened. But still, deep in my shriveled little heart, I am so proud of you."

Tamara pulled her mom close again. "Thank you, Mom."

"Don't thank me. It's only the truth. And I really am sorry for the way I behaved on the phone the other night—and just now." She sat back and whipped out another hanky to mop up the tears. "I'm looking forward to meeting Jace. I really am. And little Frankie, too."

When Jace arrived, her mom was in the tub.

He came inside carrying Frankie on one arm and food in the other.

She launched right into how Olivia had arrived out of nowhere and would be staying for an indeterminate period of time.

He set the takeout on the kitchen counter. "So, then do you want your mom to yourself for the evening?"

She eyed him sideways. "You mean, do I want you to go?"

"Well, I would understand, believe me. You haven't seen your mom in a while and—"

"Jace."

"Yeah?"

"No, I do not want you to go. I want you to stay right here with me and meet my mother." *Who had better be nice to you, or else*, she thought but didn't say.

A smile quirked the corner of his mouth. "For the night?"

"Definitely. For the night. My mom took the guest room, so you and Frankie are sleeping in my room." She gave him a look from under her lashes. "I really hope that's all right with you."

Now he was outright grinning. "Come here."

She moved in close. They kissed with the baby sandwiched all cozy between them. And then they wheeled Frankie's bassinet into Tamara's room, and Jace helped her put fresh sheets on the guest room bed.

Her mom ate lasagna and Caesar salad with them. She was on her best behavior—especially after she learned how big the Abernathy ranch was and that Jace planned to take her and Tamara out to dinner at The Association, tomorrow night.

"Tell me it's exclusive," her mother pleaded as Tamara tried not to cringe.

"You bet," Jace promised, taking her mother's snobbery in stride.

"Tiffany lamps and acres of rich hardwood, really good wines and giant fieldstone fireplaces?"

Jace grinned. "You've been there before."

Olivia laughed. "You're sharp." She winked at him and said to Tamara, "You have my permission to keep this one around."

After the meal, Olivia sat with them in the living room for a while but excused herself fairly early. "It was so good to meet you, Jace," she said, and actually seemed to mean it.

Tamara's room was pretty crowded that night, with Frankie in his bassinet and Tamara, Jace and Harley sharing the bed.

Tamara whispered, "I keep meaning to ask you who's taking care of Luna and Bailey?"

"My sisters and brothers love them. My mom and dad, too. They're taking turns looking after them."

"I kind of want you to bring them here."

"Now, that would be a full house."

"No kidding."

He nuzzled her neck. "How's your mother with dogs?"

"Not great. Maybe they should stay at the ranch, after all—for their own well-being." She kissed him. "And I think I should probably stick around here in town tomorrow with my mom."

He kissed the side of her neck, slowly, with tender care, coaxing a soft moan from her lips. "I'm a little disappointed," he said, "but I do think you're right. She needs you now. I can stay for breakfast, but then I should go home. On the Bonnie B, there's always something that should've been done yesterday. And Billy and Theo get grouchy when I don't hold up my end."

"Sounds good. Then tomorrow night, you can wow my mom with a fancy dinner at The Association."

"That is my plan." Jace pulled her closer.

"We have to be quiet," she whispered on a happy sigh.

"I'll do my best." He kissed the words onto her lips.

A few minutes later, Harley retired to the chair in the corner.

Tamara giggled at that.

Jace teasingly shushed her—and then somehow, they managed to make slow, tender love without waking the baby.

Or her mom.

In the morning, Jace sat at the table feeding Frankie his bottle and feeling damn good about everything. He and Tamara were together in that real, solid way now. They were going to make it—for a lifetime if he had anything to say about it.

Tamara stood at the stove frying bacon and flipping pancakes. This was life as it was meant to be, no doubt about it.

Olivia drifted in wearing a fancy lace robe, her thick brown hair, so much like Tamara's, loose on her shoulders.

Jace greeted her. "'Mornin' Olivia."

"Good morning, Jace." She looked tired, but she

did manage a smile as she bent over the baby. "He's a cutie—and I must have my coffee immediately." She went to the coffee maker and poured herself a mugful, doctoring it with cream and sweetener. As she was pulling out a chair at the table, the doorbell rang.

"I'll get it." Jace adjusted his hold on his son and started to rise.

"Stay right there." Olivia set down her mug. "You've got the baby and Tamara's cooking. I think I can manage to answer the door." She rose and swept from the kitchen.

A moment later, he heard her let out a cry from the other room.

Tamara heard it, too. She flipped off the burners and darted for the living area. Jace, still holding Frankie, got up and followed.

They found the front door standing open and Olivia in the arms of a tall, lean man with silver hair. "Nigel," Tamara's mom said breathlessly, "what are you doing here?"

"You left me. I came home and there was nothing but a note." Nigel tipped up her chin with a finger. "Not a very nice note, either. I chartered a jet and got here as fast as I could."

"Yes, well. I thought…"

"What?" He kissed her, hard.

When he lifted his head, she said breathlessly, "You're always working."

"I really didn't know you cared."

"Well, I do. I…" She drew a slow breath and then finally realized that Jace, the baby and her daughter had come running. "So sorry, darling," she said to Tamara. "How about if I get Nigel a cup of coffee and he and I retire to the guest room to talk?"

"Great idea, Mom. Nigel, how've you been?"

"Better now," said the older man. "Good to see you, Tamara. You must come to visit again soon." He cleared his throat and gave Jace a careful smile. "Hello. I'm Nigel."

"Jace." He stepped forward and offered his hand, and Nigel took it.

About then, Olivia reappeared with two mugs of coffee. Her cheeks were flushed, and she smiled at her husband. "Ready?"

"Lead the way."

A moment later, the two of them vanished into the short hallway that led to the bedrooms.

The front door still stood open. Harley sat on the welcome mat cleaning his long, skinny tail.

Tamara shrugged. "He's waiting for someone to chase him. It's no fun for him if I just let him go." She clicked her tongue. "Come on now. Back inside." Harley rose and strutted through the square of entryway into the main living area.

That night at The Association, Tamara couldn't have been happier.

Her mom and Nigel had patched it up. The two decided to stay the night because her mom didn't want to miss the visit to the local cattlemen's club. As they ate melt-in-your-mouth steaks and sipped fine wine, Olivia asked if there was a ballroom. Jace assured her there was. After the meal, he took them all for a tour of the clubhouse and the grounds.

"What a perfect place for a wedding," Olivia remarked as they were leaving.

Tamara rolled her eyes at that.

But Jace said, "You're right. I've been to a couple of weddings here. They were beautiful." He took Tamara's hand.

She sent him a smile, and the look in his eyes made her breath catch in her throat.

At her house, they dropped off her mother and Nigel, and picked up Frankie and Sonia. The nanny had agreed to come to town and watch the baby for a few hours.

By the time they'd driven Sonia home, picked up the dogs at Robin's house and brought them home where they belonged, it was past midnight. At Jace's place, they put a sweetly sleeping Frankie in the nursery room and entered the larger bedroom next to it.

"I can't believe we have your bedroom all to ourselves." Tamara fell across his giant bed. "This mattress is amazing. It's firm but so comfortable."

"Life is just about perfect," he said as he crossed to the walk-in closet, disappeared inside and came back out with a small velvet box.

She saw that little black box in his hand, sat bolt upright and squeaked, "Jace!"

He went to his knees at the side of the bed. "I've been waiting for weeks to say this."

She had to swallow hard to get rid of the giant lump in her throat. "But we've only known each other for a few—"

"Tamara," he said, his voice rough and low, "I knew you were the one the day after we met. I think it happened when you wouldn't let me change your tire. I saw then that you were exactly the kind of woman I'd been looking for, the kind of woman who could take care of herself—but that maybe, if I played my cards right, you might let me be the one to make sure you always got whatever you needed. You might allow me to stand beside you, working with you to make the kind of life a man can look back on with pride and gratitude."

She swiped fat, happy tears from her eyes. "Jace, I—" He was shaking his head. She didn't get it. "What?"

He commanded gruffly, "Let me say it first."

She sniffed and swiped at her eyes again. "Oh, Jace."

He opened the velvet box, removed the contents and set the box aside. "Give me your hand."

She reminded herself to breathe as she held it out to him. He clasped her fingers gently, and she melted inside at his touch.

"Tamara Hanson, you are everything I've ever wanted. And I love you with all my heart."

She couldn't hold the words back for one second longer. "Oh, Jace. I love you, too. So much!"

He held her gaze so steadily. "Tamara, will you marry me?"

"I will," she whispered. And then she said it right out loud. "Yes, Jace, I will!"

He slipped the ring on her finger, a beautiful, glittering oval diamond on a rose gold band.

"It's perfect," she said. "I love it—and I love you. So much more than I can ever say."

And then he was sweeping to his feet and grabbing her up into his big, strong arms. Laughing together for sheer joy, they danced around the room to music only they could hear, both of them knowing that whatever the future brought, they would share it together.

Side by side.

Hand in hand.

Early the next morning, someone knocked at the cabin door. Jace was giving Frankie his bottle, so Tamara went to see who it was.

She pulled open the door and there was Bonnie, looking very nervous. "Bonnie, come in."

"Thank you," Jace's mom said softly as she stepped over the threshold. She took in Tamara's robe and fuzzy slippers. "I, um, see that you and Jace have worked things out?"

"Yes, we have."

"I'm so glad."

Tamara couldn't bear it. "What's the matter? You seem nervous, and there's nothing to be nervous about."

"Yes, there is. I came to apologize for my thoughtless words last Monday. I should have kept my mouth shut, but I've never been good at minding my own business. I get pushy when I see how things should be. I get impatient for a good result. And you and Jace together, that's the best thing that could happen to my youngest son. He absolutely adores you, and you are everything he needs in a woman—in a wife."

"Bonnie, it's—"

"Wait. I'm not finished."

"Oh. Sorry. You go ahead."

"Tamara, from that first day I met you, I knew you two were a match. What you overhead on Monday was me trying to push my son to make a move, you know? But the pushing was wrong and my reasoning was manipulative. I'm so sorry and so very ashamed of myself."

Tamara couldn't hold back any longer. She grabbed Jace's mom in a hug and whispered, "I'm really glad you want to see Jace and me together—because Jace proposed to me last night."

Bonnie grabbed her by the shoulders and cried, "Make me the happiest mom alive! Tell me you said yes."

Tamara held out her left hand. "I said yes."

Bonnie gasped. "A ring! It's beautiful—and I can't

believe it. This is wonderful!" She grabbed Tamara and hugged her even tighter than before.

"Mom, settle down." Jace came out of the kitchen, Frankie in his arms.

With another gleeful cry, Bonnie went to hug him and Frankie, too. "This calls for a celebration," she announced, when she let them go. "Tonight. A family barbecue in honor of the fantastic news that one of my children has finally found the love of a lifetime."

A bit later, Tamara called her mom to share the big news with her, too. Olivia, still at the house in town, actually cried. "I'm so happy for you, my darling. I truly am. I never thought I would say this about a rancher from Montana, but Jace really is just the man for you. And I can't wait to plan you a fabulous wedding."

She and Nigel decided to stay the weekend. They came out to the ranch for the barbecue celebration of Jace and Tamara's engagement.

At Tamara's request, they brought Harley and all his cat gear along with them. Tamara wanted to introduce him to the cabin where he would soon be living—and to have him meet Bailey and Luna.

The initial contact between her cat and Jace's dogs included some hissing and more than one deep, warning growl. After that, Harley avoided the dogs, while Luna and Bailey ignored the cat. It wasn't love at first sight, but at least they were all putting up with each other.

As for Olivia and Nigel, they flew back to California together late Sunday afternoon. Before they left, Olivia told her daughter that she and Nigel were getting couples counseling.

"He doesn't want to leave me," Olivia said in wonder. "Oh, darling, I do believe he and I are going to work it out."

And then, Monday morning, not long after Jace returned from his weekly volunteer shift at the station, he got the call he'd been waiting for—the one from Frankie's social worker. It was official. Jace now had the go-ahead to formally adopt Frankie.

That night, Bonnie and Asa threw yet another big Abernathy family cookout in celebration of Frankie finding his forever family right there on the Bonnie B. Jace and Tamara could hardly believe how rich and full their lives had become.

* * * * *

Look for the next title in the
Montana Mavericks: Lassoing Love continuity
A Maverick Reborn
by Melissa Senate

On sale August 2023, wherever Harlequin
books and ebooks are sold.

HARLEQUIN
PLUS

Try the best multimedia subscription service for romance readers like you!

Read, Watch and Play.

Experience the easiest way to get the romance content you crave.

Start your **FREE TRIAL** at
<u>www.harlequinplus.com/freetrial</u>.